D0021168

Stoner & Spaz

RON KOERTGE

CANDLEWICK PRESS
CAMBRIDGE, MASSACHUSETTS

Copyright © 2002 by Ron Koertge

A segment of this novel previously appeared, in a different form, in *On the Fringe,* edited by Donald R. Gallo, under the title "Geeks Bearing Gifts."

First paperback edition 2004

The Library of Congress has cataloged the hardcover edition as follows:

Koertge, Ronald.
Stoner & Spaz / Ron Koertge. —1st ed.
p. cm.
Summary: A troubled youth with cerebral palsy struggles toward self-acceptance with the help of a drug-addicted young woman.
ISBN 0-7636-1608-7 (hardcover)
[1. Cerebral palsy—Fiction. 2. Physically handicapped—Fiction.
3. Self-acceptance—Fiction. 4. Drug abuse—Fiction. 5. High schools—
Fiction. 6. Schools—Fiction. 7. Video recordings—Fiction.] I. Title.
PZ7.K8187 St 2002
[Fic]—dc21   2001043050

ISBN 0-7636-2150-1 (paperback)

2 4 6 8 10 9 7 5 3 1

Printed in the United States of America

This book was typeset in MPerpetua.

Candlewick Press
2067 Massachusetts Avenue
Cambridge, Massachusetts 02140

visit us at www.candlewick.com

For Bianca

And for Jan, who read
more versions of this
than either of us want to
remember; and for my
colleagues in the MFA
in Writing for Children
program at Vermont
College who heard or
saw parts of this and
said smart things; for
Herb Rabbin, computer
whiz; and for Bill —
vaya con Dios.

SINCE I'VE BEEN pretty much treading water all day, the marquee of the Rialto Theatre looks like the prow of a ship coming to save me.

I limp past the cleaners, the paint store, City Scapes Furniture. I step up to the ticket booth. A real one. Out in front where it's supposed to be, not buried in some mall next to a Foot Locker.

And inside sits Mrs. Stenzgarden. Her dress has flowers on it. She single-handedly keeps the rouge trade alive. She wears huge earrings like starbursts.

"Hello, Benjamin." Her finger hovers over the red button. "One?"

"Since it's Monster Week, do I get a discount?"

She glances up from the horoscope magazine she's been reading. "I don't think I understand, dear."

"Just a little joke, Mrs. Stenzgarden. Forget it."

"How's your grandmother?"

"She's fine. I'll tell her you said hello."

"Tell her I said hello."

Right.

Ticket in hand, I make my way past the posters for Coming Attractions, lit top and bottom by dusty, flickering bulbs.

It rained this morning, so I'm extra careful, but looking down at the tiles that lead to the big double doors isn't exactly a hardship. They are a very cool turquoise and black. My grandmother walked on these tiles when she was a kid. In fact, she's on a committee that wants to preserve things like this theater, that red box office, these tiles before another mini-mall moves in selling acrylic nails, kung fu, and discount vitamins.

Inside, the lobby of the Rialto Theatre smells like butter from the Paleozoic, and so does

2

Reginald: ticket taker, popcorn maker, projectionist, owner, and manager. Reginald of the world's most awful comb-over, Reginald of the bad teeth and worse breath.

"Hey, Ben. Not a bad crowd, huh?"

"I dub thee Reginald the Optimist. Now rise, go forth into the land, and promote positive thinking for your king."

Reginald grins, showing me what looks like part of the keyboard of a tiny, decaying piano.

Maybe ten patrons lean against the wall or sink into the red, once-plush couch. I know most of them by sight. They're people who don't own a VCR and don't want to. Or if they do own one can't get it out of its box. Misfits and Luddites. Castaways and exiles. And all of us alone. Whoever said no man is an island has never been to the Rialto on a Friday night. And I can't help but wonder if I'll be here in ten, twenty, or thirty years, dragging my foot down that street I've lived on all my life toward another movie I've seen before. Thoughts like that can drive a man to drink.

I, on the other hand, buy a Dr Pepper from the Goth who works the concession stand. She has a lot of black eyeliner and a down-at-the-corners mouth that says, *How can you think of snacks when everything's so bleak?* I'm just paying her when somebody behind me hisses, "Hey, loan me a couple of bucks."

"Pardon me?" It's Colleen Minou. Everybody at King High School knows Colleen. At least, everybody who wants weed.

"I said loan me a couple of bucks." She flashes a hundred-dollar bill, then glances at the kid behind the counter. "Ms. Cheerful here is not going to break this for, like, one Jujube. I'll pay you back at school."

I dig in the pocket of my khakis. "Okay, but—"

She snatches the money and points through the smudged glass while I take in the rest of her: ripped tights, an off-kilter skirt the color of a lime snow cone, leather jacket, and over that a ragged denim vest. She tosses my two dollars on the counter. "Keep the change." Her hair is tufty and ragged. She's as pale as a girl in a poem about maidens and moonlight. Then she looks at me. "You coming?"

"In a minute." In your dreams.

First of all, no way am I gimping down the aisle during Monster Week while the lights are still on. People will think I'm part of the show. And second of all, no way am I sitting by Colleen. She is nothing but trouble.

I wait through the previews, then slip between the musty velvet curtains and into the last row. I see Colleen roaming the theater. I shrink into my seat, but she vaults my legs (oh, to vault anything just once!) and settles beside me. She shows me the yellow box of candy. "What'd you get? Let's share."

"Shhhh."

"What? There's almost nobody in here but you and me. What'd you buy?"

"Dr Pepper."

"Gimme a sip." She grabs my little cup, slurps at least half of it, and hands it back to me.

"Got anything else?"

I reach into the pocket of my windbreaker and show her the apple my grandmother made me bring.

She sneers. "No thanks, Adam."

"Can you at least talk a little softer?"

"Did you hear," she hisses, "Willard got into it with the Sixty-ninth Street Vatos?"

"When the movie starts you can't talk at all, okay?"

"Did you hear they're supposed to be bringing in dope-sniffing dogs? Did you see any dogs around school today?"

"Take it easy."

"Yeah, yeah, right. I'm a little amped." She glances around, fumbles in her purse. "I'll be right back." She heads for the side door.

"Now where are you going?"

"Like I'm going to blaze it on Main Street."

"You can't smoke marijuana in the alley."

"Why not?"

"Somebody'll see you."

"So? I'll give 'em a hit."

"I mean, they'll see you and tell somebody."

"Are you kidding? Anybody rats me out is going to have to deal with Ed. I'll be back in a minute."

"Take your stub."

"Like I know where that is."

I'm going to move, I really am. Crouch in the front row. Go into the men's room. Go home even. But I don't. And pretty soon she's tapping on the door with the classic red Exit sign above it.

I open it just enough so she can slip in, hoping Reginald won't see me, hoping I won't have to explain what I'm doing, hoping he'll believe me, because what would I do if he banished me from the Rialto?

"That's better." She slides down into a nearby seat until her knees are higher than her head. "What are we seeing, anyway?"

I sink beside her. *"Bride of Frankenstein."*

"No shit? I thought it was something about a wolf man."

"That's tomorrow."

"Whatever. Anywhere I don't have to do Ed is fine with me."

I am all of a sudden totally conscious of my body. My elbow is touching hers, and it's like being plugged into a wall socket.

Not that it's some big horndog charge, either. I don't mean that. It's the way she's talking to me. *To* me. I know what sex is. Guys in the hall talk about it. Or girls acting tough. But I only hear things, see? I get them second-hand. On the rebound. Life as an eavesdropper.

"Hey." She nudges me. "Are you nodding out on me?"

"No. I was just thinking that *Bride of Franken-stein* is as good as *The Wolf Man*. You're not, you know, missing anything."

"You've seen it?"

"Oh, sure."

"So what are you doing here?"

"Oh, I check out the way the set is dressed or how James Whale uses his camera. He was a cool guy. Gay before it was okay to be gay. His suicide note said, 'The future is just old age, illness, and pain.'"

"Are you gay?"

"No! James Whale is gay."

"Whatever." Colleen yawns. As the movie starts, she leans into me and goes to sleep.

I have to admit, for once I don't watch the camera angles or the warty villagers in the background. I concentrate on not moving, on breathing evenly, on just generally what it's like to have a girl's head on my shoulder. Any girl. Even this girl. I look around the Rialto and see two or three other couples snuggled up. But for me it's the first time. Even if it doesn't really count.

Colleen doesn't wake up until the monster gets a look at his bride and howls.

She clutches at my arm. "What's going on?"

"Elsa Lanchester is just scared. Frankenstein wants to, you know, start the honeymoon immediately."

"You're kidding."

"No, she's his bride. The doctor made her for him."

"So does he jump her bones?"

"Do you really want me to tell you?"

"It's not going to be good, is it?"

"Colleen, it's a monster movie."

"Fuck that. I'm out of here."

I always sit through the credits. I am always the last one out of any theater. I even make a point of being last. I stay in my seat until everyone else has shuffled past. Then I turn my back, too, on the comforting dark.

But this time I follow Colleen. Or try to. By the time I get out of my seat, up the aisle, and through the door, she's camped on the curb.

"Hey." She motions for me.

I try to stand up straight. I try to hold my arm so it looks like it's maybe just sprained. I try to stroll over to her.

"Don't you want to see the end?" she asks.

"I know what happens."

She pats the curb beside her. "Want to sit down?"

"It's hard for me to. And then once I'm down it's hard to get back up."

"What's that thing you've got?"

"C.P.," I say.

"Oh, yeah." She stands and brushes at the back of her tiny skirt. "At least your right hand works." She grins. "You can still jerk off."

There it is again: those eyes of hers locked onto mine. Nobody ever looks right at me. Nobody talks about my disability. Nobody ever makes a joke about it. They talk toward me and pretend I'm like everybody else. Better, actually. Brave and strong. A plucky lad.

10

"You can't, like, have an operation or anything?"

I shake my head. "But when I was little I did this Bopath technique stuff and some biofeedback and a lot of physical therapy. It could be a lot worse. Did you ever see *My Left Foot*?"

She glances at my shoe.

"No, not my left foot. *My Left Foot*. The movie. The Christy Brown story where everybody thinks the guy is a vegetable, but he's really smart and he types stuff with his left foot because it's about the only part of him he's got any control over."

"The whole movie is about him typing with his foot? That must have sold a lot of popcorn."

"Actually, it did okay. Everybody likes to see people triumph over adversity. And he had some serious C.P."

Colleen just plays with her Marlboro for a while, inhaling deep, then blowing perfect smoke rings in the still air.

"Does it hurt?"

"What? My leg?"

"Yeah. Leg, arm, the whole human unit. Does it hurt?"

"No, not really."

"So then you're okay."

"Are you kidding? While every other guy raced to grade school with his pals, I rode the little bus with kids who drooled on my shoes."

She points. "Those are fucked, by the way."

"My grandma buys these shoes, okay? She thinks if I'm well dressed, nobody will notice half of me doesn't work. I'd wear ten-dollar sneakers forever if all my toes pointed in the same direction."

"You get out of P.E., don't you?"

"Yeah, but—"

"I hate P.E. It makes my chest hurt."

At school, I'm the Invisible Man. So I'm not used to this—talking to people, I mean. But I like it.

I take a deep breath. "Did you, uh, like the movie?"

"It was okay, I guess."

"The monster and Elsa Lanchester weren't really compatible. Some critic I read said that Frankenstein and the blind hermit made the best couple."

"You read about movies?"

"Uh-huh."

"For a class?"

"No."

Colleen lights a fresh cigarette off the old one. "Are you some kind of brainiac?"

"No."

"Ever read *The Great Gatsby*?"

"Sure."

"Tell me the plot, okay? Just what happens. I'm supposed to write a report or review or something."

"Now?"

She scratches her head, using all five fingers. "You're right. Call me and tell me the plot." She digs in her purse, comes up with a gnawed-looking Bic, then writes her phone number on my wrist. I like how she holds on to me with her free hand. Grandma pats me a lot, but nobody ever touches me.

Then she yawns. A big yawn. I can see the fillings, all silver, in her molars. "I don't feel so good. Give me a ride home, okay?"

"I don't drive with, you know, the way I am. I'm waiting for . . . somebody."

"So I'll wait with you." Colleen coughs

hard, spits into the gutter, then leans to inspect it. "Man, is that supposed to be green?"

In a way, I can't wait to climb into Grandma's spotless Cadillac and get out of there. Go home and watch the late show like I always do. But I want to stand here in front of the Rialto, too. All night. And listen to Colleen. And have her talk to me.

"Is this it?" Colleen asks as Grandma oozes up to the curb. "Cool."

She opens the back door and clambers in. I make the introductions as Colleen gropes in her bag for cigarettes. I mime a big *no,* then shake my head.

"Why not? This boat's big enough to have a smoking section."

Grandma glances into the rearview mirror and asks, "Have you and Ben been friends long, dear?"

"Actually, my mom won't let me hang with Ben anymore. He does all this scary stuff like hand his homework in on time and read the assignments. I try to reason with him. I say, 'Ben. Are you crazy? You've got your whole life ahead of you.'"

All of a sudden, Colleen puts one hand on her stomach, taps Grandma on the shoulder with the other. "Pull over, okay? And I mean now."

We are barely stopped when Colleen throws up out the window. She wipes her mouth with the back of one hand. "Fuck. I better walk the rest of the way."

Getting out of a car isn't easy for me. I have to handle my bad leg like it's a big, dead python. So Colleen doesn't wait for me to be polite. She scrambles out on her own, then leans in my open window. Her breath is sour. "Call me. I mean it." Then she wobbles off down the street.

My grandma lets her forehead touch the steering wheel. "What a horrible girl," she says to the speedometer. "I didn't realize you even knew people like that."

"I don't really know her."

"Why is she acting so peculiar?"

"She's loaded."

"On drugs?"

"Not Jujubes. Not anymore, anyway."

"Why in the world did you invite someone like that into my car?"

"Grandma, we just bumped into each other at the movies. It's no big deal."

"Did she ask you for money?"

"No," I lie.

"She didn't recruit you to traffic in narcotics, did she?"

"Well, she did give me this big bag of baking soda to hold for her."

"Ben, this is no laughing matter."

"Grandma, Colleen won't even remember this tomorrow."

"Well, I'm certainly going to try and banish it from my memory."

Not me, I think. *No banishing for me.*

THE NEXT DAY IS SATURDAY. Like that matters. Like every day isn't just about identical for somebody like me.

I do my homework in about two minutes, then watch *The Magnificent Seven* on Bravo. I usually love that movie—Yul Brynner all in black like the perfect Goth parent. He and

Steve McQueen prowling the West looking for five more cowboys who are in the market for adventure.

But this time it just depresses me. Those guys—even sniveling Robert Vaughn—are everything I'm not. Not just tall and good-looking with arms and legs that work. Not just that. They at least do stuff. They get out of the house, if you know what I mean. I know they're loners, but they're loners with friends. Loners who aren't always alone. They drift off with just a nod but eventually they run into each other again in Tucson or Tombstone.

What do I have? Lunch with my grandma. And after that?

"Some prunes, Benjamin?"

"I don't want any prunes."

"Are you regular?" she whispers. "Have you been regular today?"

"I'm sixteen. When you're old enough to get a driver's license, even if you'll never get one, your grandma has to stop asking gross questions, okay?"

Then I stalk away. Oh, all right—then I limp away.

My room is just as tidy as the rest of the house: no socks on the floor, no underpants hanging from the doorknob. I look at my favorite poster, the one I wanted to put up with thumbtacks, the one Grandma had framed for me instead. James Dean looks back, clearly disappointed in me.

So I open the bottom drawer of my desk, frown at the number I transferred from my wrist, and dial.

"Is this Colleen?"

"Yeah. Who's this?"

"Ben Bancroft."

"Who?"

"We went to the movies together last night. And then you hurled out the window of my grandma's car."

"Jesus, how'd you get my number?"

"You gave it to me. You wanted to know the plot of *The Great Gatsby*. I thought you had to write a paper."

She takes some time to process this. "Oh, yeah." Then she says, "So, okay—tell me the story."

I fill her in about Nick and Daisy and Tom, the yellow car, and the green light at the end of Daisy's dock.

When I'm done she says, "Just write it for me."

"Get serious."

"I am serious, Ben. I'll never remember all that. Just do it; it only has to be, like, one page. You've got a computer, right?"

"Yeah, but . . ."

"So knock it out: why is Gatsby great, who shot who where? You know the drill."

"But that's cheating."

"Right. And . . . ?"

"I barely know you. Why should I cheat for you?"

"Because then I'll show you my tits."

THE PIT IS REALLY THE HEART OF MY
HIGH SCHOOL. Everybody turns up there
to talk or smoke or eat or just hang out. The
skateboarders like falling down the wide,
amphitheater-type steps, the stoners like lying
in the sun, the writers take turns reading from
their journals, the cheerleaders prance around
in their little orange-and-black skirts.

I find myself a spot on the top steps oppo-
site the completely vandalized tables and the
vending machines, each one in its own little jail.

I'm in a good mood. Okay, Colleen's using
me. But at least I'm in the soup, you know? In
the mix. Anything is better than lying on my
cowboy bedspread with the remote in my one
good hand.

Waiting there I feel, I don't know, an-
thropological, I guess. I just need a pair of
binoculars and a field guide to watch Ed
Dorn in his black jeans and black T-shirt
make the rounds, moving from the gangstas
in their huge pants through the Mexican
tough guys and into the Asian kung-fu fighters.
Each clique has a different handshake, and
Ed knows them all. He knows which girl's

hand to grab and rub over his shaved head, which brother to joke with, which guy's Pepsi to snatch and take a sip of, which one to lean into and whisper. Colleen walks a few steps behind. She wears knee-high silver boots and looks like someone from a different galaxy.

When Ed saunters toward his gym class, a few girls follow Colleen into the girls' bathroom. I take my book bag and lurch to one of the tables facing the exit. When Colleen comes out, I want to be the first thing she sees: sitting down I look almost normal.

I'm stationed just a few yards from the resident anarchists—both of them done up in spiked hair, boots, and bondage pants—when Stephanie Brewer walks up to them. She takes out her notebook. "Can I ask you guys some questions for the *Courier*?"

Danny looks at Robert. Robert looks at Danny. They grin.

"Can I ask about your boots? Do those white laces stand for White Power?"

They glance down. "The laces keep our shoes on, man."

"What are your outfits supposed to mean, then?"

"That we're in revolt."

"Exactly," says Danny. "We're in revolt against things like oppression."

"By whom?"

"Well, duh—the oppressors."

"I understand that," she says, "but which ones? Men oppressing women, whites oppressing blacks, straights and gays, guards and prisoners, China and Tibet?"

Robert nods. "All that, man."

She asks them to stand up and turn around then because they're both wearing white shirts with the sleeves ripped off and something drawn on the backs with Magic Marker.

"So what," Stephanie asks, "does the ghost mean?"

"It's not a ghost. It's a pirate's head, like on their flag."

Robert turns around. "It's not a pirate, man. It's a skull. That's what was on their flag: a skull and crossbow."

Danny points. "Look at your own fucking earring, man. It's a pirate."

Robert takes off his earring, makes a big deal of finding some glasses in his pants pocket, and peers through them. "It's a skull. It's got little eyes."

"Pirates have got eyes, man. Otherwise they couldn't see, like, their rum or the plank or anything."

They fall all over each other laughing.

Stephanie scowls and shakes her head. "Thanks for nothing, you jerk-offs."

She turns away and scans the Pit. I'm almost right in front of her, and she doesn't even see me. Not really. I'm just the resident spaz, invisible as the sign that says NO RUNNING, the one nobody pays any attention to.

Then she intercepts Colleen coming out of the girls' room. I can't hear what Stephanie says but I can sure hear Colleen.

"Are you nuts? Go ask somebody who gives a shit."

She's still shaking her head when she gets to me. "Unbelievable. Ed would never let me forget it if I turned up in the school newspaper with a fucking opinion."

"I was watching Ed in action. He's like Louis the Fourteenth, moving through the gardens at Versailles dispensing favors."

"Louis better watch his ass," says Colleen. "This is Ed's turf."

"I guess that big tattoo on his arm is a marijuana leaf and not an ad for Vermont in the fall."

"You got that right." She leans closer and whispers, "You got the stuff?"

"I've got the book report."

"When nobody's looking, give it to me."

"Colleen, it's a piece of paper, not a kilo."

"Like you know what a kilo is." She grabs the folded sheet out of my hand and scans it. "This'll do. Give me your phone number."

"Why?"

"So I can call you."

"Why?"

"Because I might want you to write another paper for me."

"But you haven't paid for this one. Remember?" I smile to show that I'm kidding. A little, anyway. "You're going to show me . . ." I stare at her chest. "Your, you know . . ."

"My what?"

"It's okay. I knew you weren't serious." But I point, anyway.

"I told you I'd show you my tits?" She holds up the essay. "For this?"

"Uh-huh, but it's okay. It's not that good, anyway."

"Hey, if I said I would, I will." She stuffs the page into her purse, shrugs that off one shoulder, and starts to tug at the shredded black lace she wears over an old Clash T-shirt.

"No! It's okay."

"You sure?" She reveals an inch or two of very pale skin. "Live half-nude girls. No waiting."

I retreat. "It's fine. Thanks, anyway. Really."

Who is this girl? She is out of my league. Way out.

THE NEXT DAY I find myself prowling the halls. . . . Well, I don't prowl the halls, but at least I'm in the halls. I don't just go sit in my homeroom like a fungus.

Finally I spot Colleen, this time in boots that lace up to her bony knees, ripped painter's pants, and a lacey, soiled top that looks like Madonna has been mining coal in it. I don't even get a chance to say hi before she pounces.

"Did you call my house last night?"

"Yeah. I wanted to see if you liked that paper I wrote for you, if it was, you know, okay and everything."

"Why did you talk to my mom?"

"Because you weren't home."

"She said you were the nicest guy who ever called."

"So what's the problem?"

"I don't want nice guys calling; I'm a total bitch, okay?"

"You're not, either."

"Like you know anything about me."

"I know you're honest. You said you'd do

26

something if I wrote that *Gatsby* essay, and you were going to do it."

"Oh, that. My tits aren't my best feature, anyway, but you could have at least looked at them."

"We were right in the middle of the Pit."

"So?"

"We'd get in trouble."

"So?

"They'd probably call our folks, and we'd at least get detention."

"I'm always in detention."

"I've never been."

"What? You're not just crippled, my friend. You're dead." Colleen's grin fades as she slumps against the nearest wall. Her face goes from technicolor to black-and-white.

"Are you okay?"

"I just threw up. Like, a minute ago."

"You throw up a lot."

"I'm practicing for the Olympics." She takes hold of my wrist like somebody grabbing the safety bar at Space Mountain. "Talk to me, okay?"

"What about?"

"Anything. This is not from bad acid, so spare me the big, warm dog routine. Just distract me."

I put my hand over hers, just casually, though. Like I do that sort of thing all the time. "Well, last night I watched this cool little sci-fi flick where some kid's totally fine folks fall down into this sand pit where the aliens landed; next thing you know they're not so fine. It's a fifties movie where everybody's scared of radioactivity and flying saucers. So there's a lot of sameness going around. The first suburbs and all that. Thousands of guys in gray flannel suits."

She has a can of 7UP in her purse, and she takes a swallow. "Is that all you do—squat in front of the TV?"

"Please, my life is rich and full: I also go to the movies and do my homework."

"Why do homework? I get C's for just showing up and not shooting anybody."

"Grandma wants me to go to a good school."

"Oh, Grandma. What big goals you have."

When Colleen rubs her stomach and kind of groans, I point to the green can in her hand and ask, "Want me to get you another one of those? I will if you want me to."

She narrows her gray eyes. "Ed would kill you if he caught you coming on to me."

"I would be so stoked if Ed thought that. I never came on to anybody in my life."

"Oh, bullshit. Isn't there, like, some spaz dating club or something? How about that blind chick, Doris? You guys would be perfect. She can't see you limp, and you could feel her up whenever you wanted."

"I think you're serious. Do you know who Doris is hot for? Ed!"

"My Ed?"

"Your Ed. Nobody who's disabled wants to go out with anybody else who's disabled."

"Just chill for a minute, okay? I gotta pee." She gets a good strong grip on my right arm and pushes off, tottering toward the bathroom.

I love it that Colleen touches me! And if that isn't enough, I also get to chill. I've never done that. At least no girl ever asked me to. So

I lean against the wall, sort of like the other guys. If anybody wants to know what I'm doing I can say, 'I'm chilling. What's it to you?'"

FOR A COUPLE OF DAYS I don't see Colleen. Which disappoints me. Which reminds me of why I am what I am: a bit player in the movie of life. Listed at the tag end of the credits: Crippled Kid. Before Thug #1 but after Handsome Man in Copy Shop.

Then my phone rings and I lunge for it. It has to be her. Nobody calls me. I mean that. Nobody. My answering machine probably has cobwebs in it.

Without saying hello or anything, she asks, "I was talking to some kids at school about you. What happened to your mom?"

I fall back on the bed, relieved and excited. "Nobody knows. She just split." I roll onto my side. "Turn on AMC. Check out how John Ford shoots this scene so it looks like John Wayne is about a hundred feet tall."

As I watch, I hear the raspy sound of a Bic lighter, then her quick intake of breath. "I thought John Wayne actually *was* a hundred feet tall."

"*The Searchers* is still really popular. Do you know the story? Ethan totally devotes his life to finding this niece of his that the Comanches kidnapped. I guess most people like the idea of somebody who'll just look for them and look for them and never give up no matter how long it takes."

"My father disappeared, too."

"When?"

"Like about a second after I was born, I guess. Even John Wayne couldn't find that son of a bitch."

"You don't want to go look for him ever?"

"No way. Do you want to find your mom?"

"Sometimes. Around the holidays, usually. When it's just Grandma and me and a turkey as big as a VW."

"Do you know Ms. Johnson?"

"The sociology teacher?"

"And resident feminist. She says sometimes women split because they have to. She says

31

sometimes they have to be true to themselves."

"So it's not always because some kid is dragging his foot around the house?" That's when Grandma knocks softly on my half-open door. I turn my back on her and whisper into the phone, "Looks like I better go."

Colleen whispers back, "Me, too, if I want to keep up with my regimen of self-destructive behavior."

Grandma leads me into the living room. This is never a good sign. "I hope I didn't disturb you, Benjamin."

"That's okay. I was just talking to a, uh, friend."

"How nice!"

I can almost see the exclamation point, and it means she's surprised I have a friend. I'm not getting into that.

"Did you want to talk to me?"

"Yes, I spoke to the new neighbor this morning. She seems very pleasant, and I thought it would be a nice gesture if we invited her for brunch." She holds out an envelope, one of her ritzy cream-colored ones. "It's a bit on the short-notice side, but I've got leukemia next week, then UNICEF, and before you know it the whole Tournament of Roses thing begins in earnest. Our phone number's right at the bottom in case she isn't home, but I believe she is."

"You want me to take this over now?"

"It's barely dark. I don't think she'd be alarmed." Then she looks down at my sweats, the ones she sends to the cleaners.

In old-fashioned cartoons there are always rich women looking at things through these glasses-on-a-stick. That is my grandma. She pretty much looks at everything like she has glasses-on-a-stick. Including me. Especially me.

"Would you mind changing, dear, since you're going to go out-of-doors?"

For somebody with C.P., changing clothes is no piece of cake. The good side has to help the bad side, so it takes a little while. And if I'm not careful, I'll get all my clothes off and see myself in the mirror. And that is something I try never to do.

Fifteen minutes later, I'm standing on the curb, still sweating from the struggle. God, I

33

hate getting dressed. It always reminds me of how I am.

A couple of SUVs glide by, both of them driven by the littlest mommies in the world, like there's some place called Inverse Proportion Motors and the smaller you are, the bigger the car you have to buy.

Lurching across the empty street, I wave at Mr. and Mrs. Armstrong, who sit on their porch every evening and stare at the Neighborhood Watch sign with its sinister cloaked figure.

I make my way up the walk of 1003 between borders of purple lobelia. The lights are on. Music seeps out from under the oak door.

Just in case the doorbell's broken, I tap with the little bridle that hangs from the brass horse's head. When I hear footsteps I announce, "Hi, I'm a neighbor. From across the street."

The door opens. A woman in a striped caftan says, "Yes, can I help you?" Her black hair is short and shot through with gray. She has quick-looking eyes and sharp features. If some people look smoothed by hand, this lady is machine made.

I tell her my name and why I've come.

"Marcie Sorrels." She's holding a drink with her right hand, so she sticks out the other one.

I show her my bad arm, the fingers curled into a pathetic little fist.

"Not a stroke, I hope."

"C.P."

"But not dyskinetic."

"No, spastic."

"Ah, well, you were lucky."

"That's the title of my autobiography: *Ben, the Lucky Spaz.*"

She opens the door wider. "Why don't you come inside and be hard on yourself?"

All of a sudden, I just want to throw Grandma's envelope at her feet and get out of there. *What does she know?* I think. *Who does she think she is, anyway?*

And then I wonder if I'm having a heart attack, because I've never thrown anything at anybody in my life, not even a baseball. Well, for sure not a baseball.

Where does all that emotion come from? Is it just from hanging around Colleen, who's so famous for going off on teachers she has a permanent seat in detention?

I hand over the message. Marcie opens the envelope by tearing off one end, not like Grandma, who would have pried at the flap with a silver blade.

"How do you know about C.P.?" I ask.

"I used to volunteer at the Huntington Hospital." I watch her fingers caress the notepaper. "Beautiful, isn't it? I had stationery like this"— she does this thing with her eyebrows—"in my other life. Actually, in my other other life. In any event, thank your mother, and tell her I'll be there with bells on."

"It's grandmother. I'm an orphan."

When I get back to the house, Grandma is sitting in the living room, her spine absolutely straight, the crease in her gray slacks sharp enough to cut your hand on.

"She's coming. Next Sunday, just like you wanted."

"Excellent." She pats the sofa beside her. "Sit down, dear. This will just take a minute."

Oh, man. I settle onto the dark leather.

"I'd like you to make some room in your schedule this week for the Philharmonic and the

36

new play at the Taper. It means two late evenings, but this is the kind of exposure that's good for your future."

"God, Grandma. Do I have to?"

"No. But I'd rather you did. It may be hard for you to believe, but Beethoven matters."

"Well, okay, I guess. Now can I ask you something?"

"Of course, dear."

"Do you think Mom left to be true to herself?"

My grandmother sighs. "Benjamin, we've talked about this many times. I told you, she was unstable."

"Do people do things like leave people they love because they just totally have to?"

"Besides being unstable, your mother was not a success at her chosen profession."

"It wasn't a profession. She sold real estate. It was a job."

"If you say so."

"She told me once she thought it was her fault that I'm the way I am. Because she drank martinis while she was pregnant."

"That's nonsense."

"She cried."

"Delia cried about everything."

"You could find her if you wanted to, couldn't you? I mean, there's enough money."

My grandma takes a deep breath, the kind she does in her yoga class, probably. "Have you changed your mind? Do you want to find her?"

"I think I should want to, but I don't."

She leans and pats my arm, my good arm, in that way she has that makes me want to go and get my leash and trot to the front door. "Then that's settled."

I point to my room. "Then I guess I'll—"

"One more thing." My grandma looks at the backs of her hands. "Benjamin, we're judged by the company we keep. Someone may be absolutely lovely inside but the world reacts to appearances, unfortunately, so there is such a thing as guilt by association."

"Okay."

"I'm only thinking of your future."

"Who are we talking about here?"

"Who were you on the phone with?"

"Whoever it was, it's my business."

"It was that Colleen person, wasn't it?"

"You don't even know her."

"I know she's desperate for attention, and for all the wrong reasons."

"How? How do you know? All you did was give her the third degree the minute she got in the car."

"She vomited on the side of my Seville."

"It washed right off, and I should know. You made me clean it."

Grandma reaches for her teacup. Her hand is almost as white as the porcelain. "I don't want to argue. But I'd feel remiss if I didn't say something."

"Fine, you said something." I want to leap to my feet and stride away, leaving her in my indignant wake. Instead my leg gives out and I slump back onto the couch.

"I'm certain she's the kind of girl," my grandmother says, "who is used to engaging in reckless activities. And you are naive, Benjamin. You could be easily swayed."

Oh, yeah, I think. *Reckless activities. Sway me.*

THE NEXT DAY AT LUNCHTIME I settle into the cafeteria. I pretty much always sit by myself, pretending to be engrossed in a book. Jocks wander by, their trays heaped with food. The black kids have a corner staked out. The brainiacs huddle together over by the long row of windows, and three or four girls who have babies hang out by the big double doors.

But today I'm not even pretending to read. I'm looking for Colleen. About twelve-thirty she makes her way through the line, then stumbles between the long tables in those silver boots that make her look like the stunned survivor of a downed UFO. I wave her toward me and watch her put her tray down across from mine.

"A piece of bread and a pat of butter?"

"My stomach's upset. Plus I'm a little paranoid: I think the meatloaf is talking to the peas about me."

"At least sit down. You shouldn't eat bread standing up unless you're an extra in a movie about the French Revolution."

I can hear myself showing off for her, and it makes me nervous.

She points at my plate. "God, what's that?"

"Technically they're fish sticks, but I think they're really Lincoln Logs. So I'm building a little cabin." I point to a pile of spinach. "And that will go in the barn."

"Boy, you have spent a lot of time by yourself. Guess what? Last night I watched *King Kong*."

Good. Something to talk about. "Cool. Which version did you see? The Jessica Lange or the Fay Wray?"

"It was in black-and-white."

"The one with Jessica Lange and Jeff Bridges is better."

"I would see the wrong one." She tears her bread into quarters, like it's a letter full of bad news. "Ed's not around, is he?"

"I never see Ed in the cafeteria."

"I know, he hates it. His mom makes his lunch."

"Now that's interesting. I never think about Ed even having a mom, much less one who makes a lunch."

"And he's got a little aquarium in his room."

"Stop it. You're killing me. Ed's my role model."

"You don't want to be Ed."

"Oh, yeah, I do. He's got everything: looks, body, Camaro—"

"Paranoia, no future, a rap sheet."

"How'd you guys hook up, anyway?"

"I ran with some girls who liked to party. They were older than me, you know, like seniors and dropouts. And Ed was around and some guy was hassling me one night and he took care of that and gave me a ride home. And then, like, almost the very next night we ran into each other at another party. It was raining and I got wet running to his car, so he took me to the mall and bought me new clothes and then, well, you know."

I drink some milk. "There's a scene kind of like that where Dwan falls into a mud puddle and Kong washes her off in a waterfall and then dries her by blowing on her."

"Yeah, well." She tosses a piece of bread at her tray. "In the Ed version, it was kind of the other way around."

"Why do you like him?"

Colleen shrugs. "He's got good dope."

"Why does he like you?"

She hasn't been looking at me, really. She probably hasn't been listening, either; she seems all drifty and unfocused.

But when I ask why Ed likes her—and I blurt it out before I think and if I could take it back, I would—she locks in on me. A laser stare. An apprentice gorgon.

"Because," she says, "I'll get high and do anything."

That night I don't answer the phone immediately, because I like the idea that a girl is calling me. The ringing is music to my ears.

"Just hang on," Colleen says when I pick up, "while I light this thing. And don't tell me not to. I'm not some all-star, okay? I've just got a little ice-cream habit."

"Get serious. You were loaded at lunch today."

"And you're so fucking perfect."

I shift the phone to my other ear and fall back on the bed. "I didn't say that. And, anyway, my drug of choice is celluloid."

"Yeah, what is it with all the movies?"

I sit up and drink the last of some lemonade. I try to think of a cool answer, something with the word *noir* in it, but I settle for the truth. "I was never like other kids. Obviously, right?"

"Because of your CD."

"C.P., but yeah. Like when guys are getting out their bats and gloves and stuff for spring training, I'm renting *The Natural* and *Field of Dreams*. They're signing up for tae kwon do, I settle for *Karate Kid*. Their folks take them to Raging Rapids, I watch *Water World*. My whole life was like that." I hesitate, then add the lonely verb. "Is."

"Like that."

"Yes."

"Vicarious."

"Oh, yeah!"

But she hears the surprise in my voice and busts me on it. "I also," she says, "count to twenty with my hoof if you give me treats."

"Sorry."

"I've got a fucking vocabulary, okay? When I want to."

"Yeah. Obviously."

Then we just breathe for maybe thirty seconds. Or I breathe and she smokes. Then—

"You were saying?"

I sit up on the bed, which, of course, takes a little doing. "Right. I was saying. So the vicarious stuff explains part of why I watch so many movies. But when Mom ran away from home is when I went to the hard stuff."

"Porn?"

"No. Ambient light, day for night, why a close-up here, why a tracking shot there."

"You lost me."

"I got deep into the movies. Really into them. I wanted to know how they make me feel the way they do. See, if I thought about stuff like that, I didn't have to think about why Mom kidnapped herself or if it was my fault." I take a breath.

"So now you're, like, an expert."

"Yeah, right. I'm a legend in my own bedroom."

"So you're going to make movies someday."

"I'm going to major in business. Starting at Stanford."

"That's bullshit. You should make movies if you want to make movies."

"I never said I wanted to."

"But you do?"

"I owe my grandma a lot. She takes really good care of me."

"And you're easy to take care of, right? No drugs, no tats, all A's, and you brush after every meal."

"Yeah."

"And she likes having you around. You're good company."

"I guess."

"So you're even; your turn to do what you want."

"I'll bet she doesn't think so."

"Yeah, well, tough shit for Grandma."

FOR THE BRUNCH WITH OUR NEW NEIGHBOR, I wear a shirt with a little horsie on the pocket, pressed khakis, and Bass loafers.

"You look very nice." Grandma nods approvingly.

"For a guy who took ten minutes to get his socks on."

She just checks her watch, the silver Omega she always wears with the rose-colored silk blouse. "Do you think Ms. Sorrels will be prompt?"

"Beats me."

"When we chatted she had on gardening gloves from Restoration. Did you notice if she was wearing a wedding ring?"

"Are you kidding?"

"Were there pictures in the living room?"

"Actually, yeah. One of her and some little bald guy in a yellow robe."

Just then the doorbell rings and I go to answer it. Marcie stands there cradling a bottle of wine like a baby. She wears khakis, too, kind of a blue smock, and black gardening clogs she's just hosed off because they're still shiny.

"If it isn't the orphan," she says, wiping her feet. But she has a nice smile, so I smile back.

I wait until Marcie and Grandma shake hands, then I sit on the couch. Like a good boy. Our guest roams the living room, touching Grandma's things and making all the right noises. I start thinking about Colleen. What she's doing. Who she's with. Smoking dope, probably. With Ed. And they're not sitting with their hands folded waiting for the lunch Bristol Farms delivered. Ed's probably speeding and scarfing down greasy burritos that turn into even more muscles.

"Ben?"

"Yes, ma'am."

In the kitchen Grandma opens a bottle of chardonnay (C.P. and corkscrews don't go together) for Marcie. I manage to pour the spring water Grandma likes. While I take a little relish tray into the dining room, Grandma gets the brunch together, zapping stuffed baby eggplant, portabella mushrooms, and twice-baked potatoes in the microwave. Then I help her transfer everything to platters and bowls.

As we carry things in and out, Grandma asks where Marcie went to college. Like it's a foregone conclusion that she did. Like she's that sort of person. Our kind of people.

"Pitzer." She points east, toward Pomona.

Grandma watches me sit down and unfurl a napkin. "Ben's going to Stanford, aren't you, dear."

"Yes, ma'am."

"And then where?"

"I'll take Harvard Business School for a thousand, Alex."

Marcie scrutinizes me. "You look the part, but that doesn't mean much. I looked like a dutiful wife."

That takes me by surprise. I think, *Man, I know what you mean. This is just a costume. I'm only pretending to be dutiful, too.* But before I can blurt out anything, Grandma darts into the conversation like someone catching an elevator just before the door closes. "Do you live alone?"

"I'm divorced."

Grandma looks down at her perfect fingernails. "I'm sorry." Then she fingers the damask tablecloth.

Marcie takes a long swallow of wine. "Don't be. I wasn't merry enough for Tom, so we agreed to go our separate ways."

That stops Grandma for a second. Then she rallies. "How do you stay so thin, dear?"

"I have to watch what I eat. I had bypass surgery before I was forty." Marcie touches her smock. "I look like the bride of Frankenstein under here."

Reaching for some parsley potatoes, I say, "That was just down at the Rialto."

Marcie nods. "I know; I saw it. I love that actress with the original big hair."

"Elsa Lanchester. Do you like the movies?"

"Enough to make one. Or to try, anyway."

That makes me stop chewing. "You're kidding."

Marcie sits back. "When Tom left me I had one of those episodes that some call a dark night of the soul. So I did two things: I prayed and I took classes. I now know the difference between a sestina and a villanelle; I can tell a Warhol from a Lichtenstein, and I can use a Sony three-chip."

"What kind of movie did you make?"

"A little documentary. About people who'd had heart transplants. I was in Cedars recovering from this"—she points to her chest again—"when I heard these two middle-aged men talking. One of them said, 'I hope I didn't get some queer's heart. I don't want to start looking at sailors.' And the other one said, 'I was thinking maybe I got mine from some Chinese kid, because all of a sudden I can balance my checkbook.'"

"And you made a movie about that?"

"Uh-huh." She drains her glass of wine. "When the teacher told us to start thinking about a semester project, I remembered those two men. Their new hearts meant a new life for them. But it sounded to me like they were still operating inside the traditional norms of class and gender.

"I thought I'd investigate that. All I had was a bypass, and I couldn't be the same afterward. I didn't want to be the same. I wanted to know if that was unusual. So I talked to a lot of people, shot the whole thing in about a month, and edited it on my iMac. Got a B minus."

"Can I see it?"

She waves half a roll at me. "Oh, I don't think you want to do that. It's not very good."

"I don't care. I never knew anybody who actually made a movie before."

"Well, you're in luck. Tomorrow night at Caltech my teacher is showing his new class three or four of the films from last semester."

"And one of them is yours?"

"Uh-huh. I don't know if mine's an example of what to do or what not to do, but you could come if you wanted to. The class is just Basic Film Techniques, Ben. Don't expect too much."

"Let's go, Grandma, okay?"

She presses her thin lips with a napkin. "I'm afraid I have AIDS tomorrow night. But you may go, Benjamin."

I'm supposed to be getting Marcie's coffee, but I dart (well, you know what I mean) into my room and call Colleen instead. "My neighbor made a movie, and I want to see it. Go with me, okay?"

"If Ed finds out, he'll kick your ass."

"You know, I think we're more liable to see somebody walking a Chia Pet than we are to see Ed at Caltech."

I hear her cross the kitchen linoleum, hear the refrigerator door open, then the hiss of a soda can. "What's the movie about?"

"It's a documentary. That's pretty much all I know. And it's tomorrow night."

"I thought nice boys like you were supposed to call at least a week in advance."

"If you go, I'll bring you a single rose, okay, but half-dead so it'll go with your tattoo that says Born to Lose."

"Very funny."

"Go with me and I'll say more funny stuff. Your sides will ache from laughter."

I hear her inhale before she says, "This is not a date."

"I know that."

"This is a good deed, okay? I'm helping the handicapped."

"Whatever you say."

"I'll pick you up. Where do you live?"

IN THE MOVIES, usually bad ones, when somebody goes on a date, there's almost always a Changing Scene. Somebody in front of a mirror, clothes everywhere. Or popping out of a closet, each time in a different outfit.

I don't do that. For one thing, all my clothes are pretty much the same: preppy. For another, I'm ready for something a little more radical.

I'm on my way out the door for my non-date, when Grandma stops me.

"What happened to your hair?"

I take off my cap. "I stopped by Supercuts. They bleached it. And cut it a little."

"But why?"

"I just wanted to look different."

"There's different and then there's peculiar. A cat and a dog are different; a cat is not a peculiar dog."

"If you're saying I was a dog before and now I'm a cat, that's fine by me."

"It was an analogy, Ben."

"I know what an analogy is, Grandma, and it wasn't a very good one."

"There's no reason to be rude."

I let my backpack drop to the floor. "Oh, Grandma, all I did was make my hair different."

"Don't you have enough to contend with without making yourself more conspicuous?"

"It's my hair."

"But it's in my house."

"Fine, I'll leave my hair outside. Or at least put it out at night like a cat. If we had a cat. Which we don't since Mom left, because of your precious furniture. Man, I can't believe you gave away Mittens."

"The cat was unhappy without your mother."

"I was unhappy without my mother. Did you think about giving me away, too, or did I just not shed as much?"

Grandma settles onto a Stickley chair and looks down at her folded hands. I look up at the light fixture.

Then I turn to my grandmother. "Let's not fight, okay? You don't like my hair. Fine. I know that; I even understand it. But I'm not going to change it back."

"This is very upsetting. It's that Colleen person, isn't it?"

"What does that mean?"

"Remember that absurd video you made me buy for your ninth birthday, that *Devil Girl from Mars?*"

"Is that what you think Colleen is?"

"It's not that far-fetched. That character, that . . ."

"Nyah."

". . . came down to Earth to get men for her planet. And that awful girl is after you."

"I wish."

By the time I get out to the car, Colleen is standing on the passenger's side of her beat-up convertible with the door open. I try not to stare at the tattoo on her stomach—a mushroom with a dazed-looking elf on top of it.

I point at the door. "I'm the one who's supposed to be helping you."

"And you would, too, if I was the spaz."

It's funny how different that sounds when Colleen says it; it's not so much a name as a fact. Or maybe coming from her, it isn't like the brickbat people usually hurl at me.

I turn sideways, fall back into the seat, and haul my gimpy leg in as Colleen walks around to her side. The tiny skeletons hanging from both ears dance.

She turns the engine over and glances at me. "You okay?"

I reach for the ratty-looking seat belt. "Yeah."

"I was going to suggest we rob a bank, but you're not exactly up for the quick getaway."

"Tell me about it."

"Cool hair, by the way."

"My grandma hates it."

"Isn't that the point?"

We park on San Pasqual Avenue, walk half a block or so, then turn into the campus. The first girl we pass has broccoli-green hair and a T-shirt with Black Uhuru on it.

"I know her," Colleen says. "I sold her some dope." Then she puts her hand on my arm.

"Speaking of dope, is anybody around?"

"Not really. Why?"

Her right hand dives into her purse and comes up with what is almost for sure the dead end of a joint.

"You're not going to smoke that, are you?"

"I thought I might."

"Somebody might see."

"That's why I asked you if there was anybody around!" She leads me to a bench, fires up her yellow Bic, takes a hit, then offers the joint to me.

"Are you kidding?"

"Don't tell me you never wanted to."

I glance around warily. "I don't even know how to smoke a regular cigarette."

"Sip at it. And let some air in to, like, water it down."

I take the joint from her. "If I cough, don't laugh at me."

"I can't believe you're such a lightweight."

"I've led a sheltered life."

I inhale just a little.

"Hold it in," Colleen advises. "And don't talk for a minute."

I settle back, or try to settle back. When I saw *Reefer Madness,* half the people in the audience were stoned and except for a big concession stand run on Hershey's Kisses, they seemed none the worse for it. So I am pretty sure I'm not going to climb the bell tower just to get closer to the planets that are sending me coded messages. Still, this isn't like me. I study, I go to the movies, I play cards with my grandma.

When Colleen nods, I exhale.

"Well?" she says.

"Wow."

"Ed always has really good shit."

I lean toward her. "Should we do it again?"

"If you don't mind being late to the movie."

When she holds out her hand to help me up, I take it. While we walk, she links her arm through mine. My good one.

"Are we strolling, do you think?"

She laughs. "What?"

"I don't feel so clumsy. And I've always wanted to stroll. Man, why didn't my physical therapist tell me about this stuff?" All of a sudden, I stop. "Listen to that?"

"What, the air conditioning?"

"Dad used to say it was the sound of people thinking." I point. "There's the library where he worked. Did I tell you I think he killed himself?"

"I heard he drove off Angeles Crest."

"Maybe on purpose. He was really unhappy."

"After your mom split."

"And before. When they'd argue, I'd hear stuff."

"Like what?"

"Like Mom would say, 'I can't live like this. I try. I even want to, but I can't.'"

"What couldn't she live like?"

That's a good question.

"Who knows? Maybe Grandma's right and Mom was just unstable, because sometimes she was really fun. Other times she would just, like, go to her room. It was always Grandma who drove me to therapy and pretty much took care of me."

By this time we're right beside Kennedy Hall. Marcie's classroom is on the first floor, but before we go in, I stop Colleen.

"That stuff we smoked is great. Why is it illegal? I feel fantastic."

Inside, maybe twenty-five people chat or flip through their textbooks. The teacher is a guy with a big Walt Whitman beard. He shuffles through a dozen video cassettes.

When Marcie sees us, she waves and heads our way.

"Ben! You made it, and you brought your new hair. Where's Grandma?"

"Fundraising. For AIDS, remember?" I tug at Colleen. "Oh, say hi to Colleen. She's got a boyfriend, so we're just pals. Barely friends. In fact, it's some sort of deviation in the time-space continuum that we're even in the same room together."

Colleen holds out her hand. "Hi. Don't pay any attention to him."

"Sit in the back. I'm second, so you can slither out after mine if you want."

We settle into the chairs, me with my good side next to Colleen. The teacher gives a little speech, thanks his former students for letting him use their videos, then slips in the first one, which is a Claymation-style film called *Kiss Me Till I Melt*.

It opens with two clay figures face to face; then the filmmaker irises in to show us some time has passed. Scene two shows them lying on top of each other. More irising in. In scene three, you can't tell who's who anymore. There's just a big lump of clay.

Nervous laughter. Lights up. Applause, applause.

Then Marcie's movie starts. A lady sits in a lawn chair outside one of those giant motor homes. She wears a kind of white coverall, sunglasses, and a baseball cap with NASCAR on it.

"We were on our way from Michigan to Texas Motor Speedway when Bobby just up and died on me. I was driving and he was supposed to be taking a nap. We just happened to be going through St. Louis when he came up behind me and said, 'Sweetheart, I don't feel too good.' And those are the last words I heard him say."

She reaches for a tall glass of iced tea. "Hell, we just liked to follow the stock cars: Little E,

Dale Jarrett, Mark Martin, and those boys. But the fella who got Bobby's heart likes to read books and grow vegetables. Don't you think that'd be like going to sleep in the middle of Speed Week at Daytona and wakin' up in Leisure World?"

Even Colleen laughs and sits up a little straighter. I scoot forward in my seat because I like this little movie. Also, I feel really good.

Marcie uses an establishing shot next: the Altadena sign at the city limits, then a street named Poplar, then a little living room with big furniture and a tiny woman dressed all in green like an elf.

"I don't have much to say. Mark was playing football in the street when a car hit him. The boy who got his heart was also named Mark. For a while I heard from him real regular. Then not so often. Then only at Christmas. And lately not at all." She rubs the edge of the coffee table. "He's just a boy. Mark is. The live one. Boys get distracted easily. I know that for a fact."

That's when Marcie splices in some stock operating room footage: the chest cracks and opens, some doctor's gloved hands probe, a big bloody sponge balances on the sternum.

"Oh, gross!" Colleen buries her face in my shoulder.

I've seen this a hundred times. Not the stuff on the screen, but a girl hiding her eyes, her hair against some boy's neck the way Colleen's is against mine. His comforting arm around her shoulders, the way mine is.

"Is it over?" Her warm breath seeps through my Brooks Brothers shirt and into my skin.

"Uh-huh."

Marcie opens with a slow pan across a McDonald's menu, goes close on a bin of French fries, then across some Big Macs all wrapped up in their swaddling clothes. The camera settles on a big guy in a white T-shirt tearing into a Quarter Pounder. He never stops eating while he says, "I went to the interview with the transplant people right after my doctor found what he found, but when I heard, 'Trade death for a lifetime of medical management,' I said the hell with it. I'm not going through all that heartache just to eat tofu and rabbit food and have somebody stick me with a needle nine times a week." Then he cocks his head. "Did I say heartache? I meant hassle."

This time Marcie splices in footage from some monster movie, the scene in the inevitable laboratory where a heart lies throbbing under a bell jar while mine, when Colleen leans into me and closes her eyes, races like mad.

When the movie is over, everybody applauds, this time like they mean it. While the teacher is switching cassettes, Marcie signals for us to meet her outside.

"What happened to those old guys?" I ask. "The ones you told me about at brunch, the ones in the hospital who were afraid their hearts were going to make them gay or Chinese?"

Marcie shrugs. "They were just garden-variety racists. On camera, they were way too polite to be interesting."

"The totally cool thing," I say, "is that you made that all by yourself."

"Pretty much. I picked up the iMovie program for my Mac, but that was about it. I'm probably not going to use it again."

"Why not?"

Marcie shrugs. "I start things and then don't finish them."

"You finished your movie."

"I guess. But I don't feel like doing another one. If you're interested, I could show you, though. Why don't you both come over sometime?"

I glance at Colleen, who says, "I don't think that'd be a real good idea."

Just like that I'm not as happy as I was. And maybe that's what weed does: lifts you up, then drops you like a careless parent.

"Well, it's a standing offer." She squints at the bright lights in the dingy corridor. "You are made for black-and-white, Colleen. She looks like Helena Bonham Carter. Doesn't she, Ben?"

"In *Fight Club*."

"Exactly."

When Marcie says goodbye and goes back to watch the rest of her classmates' movies, I take a deep breath. "Man, I loved that."

"Who's Helena Bon Bon Carter or whatever her name is?"

"A British actress. In a lot of Merchant/Ivory movies."

"Is she pretty?"

"Oh, yeah."

"Was she pretty in *Fight Club*?"

I push open the double doors and we step out into the evening. "For sure, in a kind of edgy, ruined way."

"Cool." All of a sudden Colleen stops. I can feel her sharp, black nails through my shirt.

"What?"

"Those cops."

I glance at two campus policemen in khaki uniforms strolling our way. "What about 'em?"

"They're going to hassle us."

"Are you kidding? They're just a couple of guys making eight fifty an hour."

Colleen shoots me a glance of pitiless scorn.

"Evening, folks," says the taller cop.

I read their name tags: Ketchum and Chu. It sounds like some horrible restaurant.

Colleen advises me not to say anything. "You don't have to. This is public property. They've got no probable cause."

Officer Chu smiles. "Maybe a little less of the *Law & Order* marathon and a little more sleep?"

Colleen crosses her arms.

Officer Ketchum's lapel radio crackles. A static-riddled voice says something about Dormitory C.

As they turn away, Officer Chu touches the brim of his cap in a lazy salute. "Have a pleasant evening."

"We were, till you showed up."

Ketchum says something to his partner, and they both laugh.

Colleen watches them disappear around the corner of a tall, ivy-covered building.

"What was that all about?"

Colleen sighs. "Come over here." She leads me to a bench, half-hidden by a drooping eucalyptus tree. She sits down, rummages through her purse, then lights another joint. Which she holds out to me.

"Just this once," I say, trying to keep things light. But I also want to feel like I did an hour ago.

"I've got this thing about cops, okay?"

"Because of Ed?"

"That and Mom had a boyfriend who was a cop, and he was a total creep."

I hand her the cigarette. I like the way the lamppost all of a sudden looks like a dandelion.

"This is in North Dakota, okay?"

"You and your mom and this cop?"

"Yeah. I was ten. And Ralph lived with us. Big son of a bitch. Worked out all the time. Then one night he comes into my bedroom, okay? And starts rubbing my back. How am I? How was school?

"I had this little light with, like, angel cut-outs and it spun, you know? When the bulb got hot? So there's these angels' shadows on my pajamas while I'm telling him about my math test, and all of a sudden he starts rubbing my legs." She sucked on the joint. "I'm fucking terrified. He's huge. His hands are, like, giant. So I get up and go in the bathroom and I stay there until I hear him walk past, and then I go back to bed and lay there all night afraid to go to sleep."

When she holds out the smoke, I shake my head and reach for her hand instead, but she pulls it away.

"Next morning, I tell my mom. She freaks."

"She should."

"But not about Ralph. About me. I'm imagining things. He was just trying to be nice. I just don't want her to be happy. And I think to myself: *I'm on my own.* I'm fucking ten years old, and I'm on my own."

Colleen dives into her purse again, this time surfacing with a little amber-colored vial. Using a silver spoon so tiny it could've come from a dollhouse, she snorts what has to be cocaine. Now I'm getting nervous.

"So what did you do?"

"Split."

"You ran away from home?"

"Not very far, just up the street to my girl-friend's house."

"But he was there the next night, right?"

"I didn't go home then, either. There was always someplace to stay, you know? Somebody's parents are always gone. This one girl lived in her parents' garage, and I crashed with her for like a week."

"Your mom didn't care?"

Colleen shrugs. "I called home. I said I was sleeping over." She taps on the little glass bottle with the spoon.

"So what finally happened?"

"Ralph took off. My mom's boyfriends always take off."

She reaches into her purse, lights up, and inhales like she's a diver about to go as deep as she can for as long as she can.

"Do you think you're the way you are," I ask, "because of stuff like that?"

"Meaning what?"

"Colleen. You're a drug addict."

"Bite me. I smoke a little. I snort a little coke. Big deal. You should watch who you're calling names. You're this fucking loser who limps."

I look down, appropriately enough, at my shoes. One's fine, the other's worn down on one side and all scuffed up.

I try not to let my voice shake. "I didn't

mean just you. I meant me, too. Am I a loser because my mom left and my dad died? My therapist used to say that people spend their whole lives getting over stuff their parents do, even nice parents."

Colleen stands up. "That's bullshit."

She's so loud that a couple of guys walking by stop and stare. I tug at her ice-cold wrist.

She sits down again but pulls her hand away and hisses, "That's bullshit. Maybe I'm a stoner, but the devil doesn't make me do it and my mommy and daddy didn't make me do it."

When she fills the little spoon another time, I scoot to the left so I'm more between her and people on the sidewalk. "Take it easy, okay? My dad used to work here."

"Where were you when I needed a non sequitur for Mrs. Hamilton's class? What's your dad got to do with anything?"

"I used to know people. They might recognize me."

"That was years ago."

"I still limp."

"You're sitting down, for Christ's sake."

I struggle to my feet, never a pretty sight. "Let's talk about this tomorrow, okay?"

"You started it. You want to blame your mom and dad because you're a snob, go ahead. But it's bullshit."

"A minute ago I was just a loser. Now I'm a snob, too?"

"Well, what do you call a guy who never talks to anybody?"

"Hey, nobody talks to me."

"And that's somebody else's fault?"

"I'm a spaz, in case you haven't noticed."

Colleen holds out her hand and lifts a finger for every name: "Don Secoli is in a wheelchair, and he's Mr. High School. Karen Radley's practically deaf, and she still plays drums in some garage band. Doris Schumacher's blind, but all you have to do is say one word to her and she knows who you are. Get over yourself, okay?"

I lean in. "Will you not rant, please? People are looking at us."

"Oh, who cares."

"I care. You've got a purse full of drugs."

"Ed will bail us out. All you'll get is probation for a first offense."

I tug at her, draw her deeper into the shadows. "I don't want Ed to bail me out; I don't want probation; I don't want to go to jail, period." Then I watch her light another joint. Her purse is like something from a fairy tale, one of those magic sacks that's never empty. "Aren't you high enough?"

She takes a gargantuan hit, then offers it to me. I wave it away as she says, "I never get high enough."

With each word, out comes a little puff of smoke like those ominous signals the settlers saw when they crossed into Indian territory.

When I hear people behind us whispering and snickering, I turn on them. "What are you looking at?" I demand. "There's nothing to see, okay?" Then I lean against the nearest tree.

Colleen fiddles with the joint she's just lit, stares at it, inhales a little smoke by passing it under her nose like some plutocrat with a

Havana cigar. Then she flicks off the lit end and drops the rest back into her purse. "I'd better lie down," she says, sinking onto the lawn. "I've kind of got the whirlies."

I go and stand over her, half-mad and half-worried. "Are you sick?"

"Maybe sit by me for a minute. I'll be okay."

I lower myself onto the damp grass, which takes a little doing. "I can call a cab if you want. You shouldn't drive."

"Just give me a minute. I'll be fine. I'm used to this."

"Why do you do it?"

Colleen props herself up on both elbows. "Oh, I don't know. There's a point where I'm just about perfect: just high enough but not too high. Everything makes sense to me, or if it doesn't, I don't care. So I guess I figure if I feel this good on a few hits, I'll feel twice as good on twice as many. Stupid, huh?"

"Kind of."

She sits up then and rubs my arm. The nearest one. The withered one. I flinch, but she doesn't seem to notice. "I'm sorry I called you a snob."

She's not looking at me, so I'm not looking at her. Yet. But her bare hand on my skin feels out of this world. "I'm sorry I called you a drug addict."

She lets her hand slide down to my fist then, because that's what I have on that side. A permanent fist. "I know I smoke too much."

"I don't try hard enough. I should talk to people more."

Colleen leans into me then. She puts a hand on my cheek. "I like your hair."

"Man, you are loaded."

"It's cute. You're cute."

"If you pet me," I say, "I'll follow you home."

"Yeah? What'll you do if I kiss you?"

I don't know what to say to that. I can't think of a thing. You have to remember: I've been a spaz all my life. I never kiss anybody. Nobody ever kisses me.

Colleen murmurs, "My science teacher is always saying, 'Try. You won't know what a combination of elements will do unless you try.'" She leans closer. Her breath is heavy and sweet. "What's the worst that could happen, huh?"

I think, *I could explode and then you'll wish you'd worn your safety glasses.* But I don't say that. I don't say anything. I'm getting ready for this kiss. I'm licking my lips, because that's what people do in the movies, and I've seen a million of those.

About an hour later, I ease through the front door and close it behind me. I'm as stealthy as Tom Cruise in *Mission: Impossible.*

"Ben? Is that you?"

But, apparently, not stealthy enough. I sigh. "Yes, Grandma."

"Can you come in here a minute, dear?"

I lurch down the hall (either making out or smoking dope seems to have made my limp worse, but it was worth it), pause outside the door, and smooth down my new hair. Colleen doesn't wear lipstick but I rub my mouth on my sleeve, anyway.

When I step inside, my grandmother is tucked into her narrow bed like a knife slipped into a sheath.

"Did you have a good time?" she asks. "Was the movie interesting?"

"It was fine. What's wrong, Grandma?"

"I'm afraid I'm ill, Benjamin. Will you get the thermometer?"

In the medicine cabinet everything has its place: cleansing cream here, nail clippers there. One blue toothbrush hangs beside a spotless drinking glass.

I shake down the thermometer with my good hand.

"Did you cleanse it with alcohol?" Grandma asks.

I stare at the thermometer. I'm still a little high. The mercury is beautiful. "Did I cleanse it? No, it was in its little house so I figured . . ."

"Cleanse it, dear."

"Grandma, this isn't Russia, where there's one thermometer for all of Moscow."

"Benjamin, please."

I plod to the sink and run some hot water. Back in the bedroom, I thrust the slender glass cylinder under her tongue.

"Iz ust aim on," she said.

"Grandma, don't talk."

She waves the thermometer like a tiny baton. "This just came on. One minute I'm fine, happily listening to a very nice young man in a beautiful Armani suit talk about opportunistic infections; the next I'm woozy and flushed."

"Grandma, stop talking. I'll be back in a minute."

In my bedroom, I pick up the phone and stare at it; even it's pretty, light reflecting off its ivory surface. Then I dial Colleen's number. It's busy.

"Ben. Come and read this, please. I must have left my glasses in the kitchen."

Back in the room I squint and say, "A hundred and two."

"Oh, god, I've got influenza."

"Probably. A lot of kids at school—"

"It's different for an elderly person."

"You're not elderly."

"What if it goes to my chest? I've always had weak lungs."

"You've never had weak lungs."

"I don't tell you everything, Ben. I don't want you to worry."

"You went to the doctor and he said you had weak lungs?"

"I don't need a doctor to tell me I can't hold my breath as long as I used to."

"When do you hold your breath? You don't dive for pearls; you talk to your broker."

"Sometimes when I'm here alone, I test my lung capacity."

"What a picture that is."

"I'm glad you're home safely. Anxiety can undermine one's immune system."

"Colleen just gave me a ride to the movie and back."

"She has an eye tattooed on the palm of her hand!"

"Just a little one."

"She's dangerous."

"You don't know her, Grandma." I sway a little, then sit down heavily on the edge of the bed.

My grandmother tries to sit up. "Are you all right, dear? You aren't getting sick, too, are you?"

"I'm hungry. I'm really hungry. Have we got any cookies?"

FOR TWO DAYS THIS IS WHAT I HEAR: "Ben, could you warm this tea up just a little, please? Not too much, though. My tongue feels peculiar already." "Ben, may I have a glass of water? And not from the tap, dear." "Ben, will you rewind *The Sound of Music* and start it again? And then sit and watch with me for a little while."

Or variations thereof. So I'm glad to go back to school. I'm peering into my backpack when Colleen appears. I can't tell her that I missed her. She's not that kind of girl.

So I say, "Did you get my message?"

"Yeah, Granny was sick. Thanks for checking in. I didn't call you back, I figured . . ."

"Yeah."

"You look kind of fucked up."

"Haven't you heard? The hills are alive with the sound of music." I lean against the wall, which is painted the color of grasshopper guts. I look over Colleen's shoulder, then my own. A lot of kids carry their books in those black luggage carriers with little wheels: flight attendants to nowhere. "You okay?"

"I've been baby-sitting, too. Mom got collagen in her lips and something went wrong so she looks like Daffy Duck. I hung out with her and we watched a really cool movie on cable where this totally cute cowboy can't keep his hands off this chick named Pearl."

"That's *Duel in the Sun* with Gregory Peck and Jennifer Jones. He's Lewt McCanles and she's Pearl Chavez, the fiery half-breed."

"That was hot. Made my mom's lips throb."

"I used to practice flicking my cigarette away like Gregory Peck, because in the movies, girls always go for the bad guys."

"You don't smoke."

"I used a Tootsie Roll miniature."

"You're kind of far-out in your own weird way, you know that?"

"Really?"

"I like the way you argue, too. I say I'm sorry I called you a name, you say you're sorry you called me a name, and that's that. When Ed and I get into it, he pouts for about a week."

I step closer. "Look, let's go over to Marcie's."

"I don't know, Ben."

"Oh, c'mon. I just want to see her camera."

Colleen shakes her head. "Making out when I'm loaded is one thing; making social calls is . . . I don't know. Doesn't one of us have to wear pearls for shit like that?"

"It's not a date."

"It wasn't a date the other night, and I ended up with my tongue down your throat."

"Like you said, you were loaded. So leave your stash at home. I think totally sober you'll find me pretty easy to resist."

"I don't get you sometimes. What do you want with me, anyway?"

"I want you to go to Marcie's with me."

She looks down at her black fingernails. "Let me think about it."

"I'll call her after school. Then I'll call you."

I'M WATCHING FOR COLLEEN, so by the time she parks, I'm right there at the curb.

"I'd ask you to come in and say hi to Grandma, but she's already in bed. That flu really got her good."

Colleen grimaces. "That's okay, especially if this is the same Grandma whose car I threw up in."

"Actually, you threw up out the window."

"Oh, well. Then she could see I'd been brought up right."

I point to Marcie's house. "Ready?"

"I did what you said—I left the weed at home."

We let a couple of cars go by, then start across the street. "So how is it?"

"I've been straight before. I can't recommend it as a lifestyle, though." A hot, dry wind off the desert nudges Colleen's hair and even the purple lobelia lining Marcie's walk.

When we get to the porch, Colleen stops. "What am I supposed to do, anyway, while you go to film school? I'm gonna have to talk to her."

"Grandma says to ask questions."

"Things like, 'Say, Marcie, that's a nice rack for an old lady. Are they real?'"

I slump against her. Accidentally. On purpose. "That sound you hear is the blood draining from my face."

The door opens almost before I can knock, and we step inside. A little fountain that I don't remember from the first time I was over stands in the foyer; water trickles off a tiny ledge and into a bowl-sized pool.

Marcie's wearing overalls and a blue T-shirt. I can see her bare feet as she points at nothing in particular and says, "Take a look around."

Colleen and I amble through the living room like museumgoers. There are a lot of books, and on the walls long scrolls decorated with big Chinese-looking letters.

Colleen picks up a little pile of old-looking coins. "Souvenirs?"

"Oh, that's feng shui stuff. Those and the fountain and the mobiles."

"What's . . . whatever you just said?"

"Oh, I dabble in things. A little meditation, a little prayer, a little tai chi, and in this case a little bit of the way of the wind and water." She points toward the kitchen. "Can I get you something to drink?"

When we're alone for a minute, I say, "Nice house, huh?"

Colleen nods. "She didn't buy this place making documentaries." Then she nudges me. "How am I doing? Did you hear me say, 'Souvenirs?' Granny would've been proud."

Marcie drinks red wine. Our Cokes are in milky-looking blue-and-white glasses. Colleen takes a big gulp, plucks a picture off the piano, and says, "Who's the little guy in the robe?"

"One of the Buddhists I studied with when I was in Tibet."

When a breeze rustles the scrolls on the wall, Colleen asks, "What do Buddhists do? They don't go to church like regular people, do they?"

Marcie folds her napkin. "When somebody asked a monk what went on in the monastery, he said, 'We fall down and get up, fall down and get up.'"

Colleen grins. She's beautiful. "I guess they're not just clumsy."

"They might be that, too, but mostly he meant they're not too hard on themselves when they screw up. Mostly Buddhists pay attention to the Four Noble Truths, only two of which I can remember at any one time."

It's my turn: "What are they today?"

"If you're alive you suffer, and there's a reason for your suffering."

Colleen sets the picture down. "Those zany Buddhists. Always kidding around."

"I know it sounds grim." Marcie stretches extravagantly. "But Buddhists are probably the happiest people I've ever met. Every time I sat down with my teacher he warned me about wasting this incarnation, and all the time he's got this huge grin on his face."

This time Colleen doesn't sound so cocky. Maybe nobody would hear it except someone like me who has sat in the dark for years listening to dialogue. "So," she asks, "were you wasting this incarnation?"

"I still haven't figured that one out. I flit a lot, you know—here, there, hospice work one year, classes at Caltech the next." She offers

Colleen more Coke out of a big blue pitcher full of ice. "What do you guys see at school? Are kids passionate about things? Ben's in love with movies. What are you in love with, Colleen?"

Colleen and I look at each other. She shrugs before she says, "I used to write letters to the President."

"What about?"

"Saving trees, mostly. I was, like, really nuts for trees."

"Are you still involved in the movement?"

Colleen finishes her drink. "I, uh, kind of got distracted. I still have a thing for plants, though. Some plants, anyway."

That's my cue to change the subject. "How about a little toast?" I say. "To the person who made *Meandering Hearts,* a very cool movie."

Colleen raises her Coke. "I'll drink to that."

Marcie takes a long swallow of wine. "Wasn't it amazing how some of those people really valued their new hearts and kind of babied them by losing weight and eating right and all? And then others were just like, 'Okay, now I can have all the lard sandwiches I want.' I mean, they had a chance to change their lives and they didn't take it!"

The Tibetan scrolls undulate again, but there isn't a breeze. The hair on my arms stands up. I wonder if Marcie is talking about me, too.

Colleen puts her glass down, careful to keep it on the woven coaster. "How long did it take you to make the whole movie, anyway?"

There it is again. When we first sat down it was like Colleen was reading questions off note cards. But now she really sounds kind of curious.

Marcie frowns as she does a little math in her head. "Oh, a couple of months, I guess. But a lot of that was logistical: tracking people down, getting to where they were. I sure shot a ton of film I didn't use. But that's part of it. If people are too nervous, it's no good. If everybody's real slick, the whole thing looks rigged. They had to trust me, you know? They had to feel that I wasn't going to exploit them for my own ends." She reaches over and pats my arm.

"You should make one of your own."

"Yeah, right. The only things I know anything about are my grandma and the movies."

"You should do high school," Colleen says. "Call it *Weirdos Galore*."

Marcie stands up. "That's a good idea. Let me show you the wonders of iMovie. Maybe you'll get inspired."

In the study, Marcie reaches into a drawer and comes up with a small camera. "I can loan you this old Sony. It's analog, okay? But don't worry about that. I've got an adapter that'll digitize it so we can feed it right into the iMac and edit it. Then we'll turn it back into analog so we can play it on a VCR."

"Say that in English."

"For right now, shoot a minute or two of film." She offers me the camera.

"If you need two hands for this, there goes my new career."

"One'll do."

I put my fingers, the ones that work, through the strap on the side. "So what should I shoot—you?"

"Me. The room. Colleen. It doesn't matter."

I try peering through the viewfinder. "Like this?"

"That's all there is to it. Now push that button."

Easier said than done. "I can't."

"If you have to, rest the camera on your bad arm."

"It won't go that high."

"Try putting the camera on the desk. Then push the button."

So I do what she says. "Is it working?"

"Is the red light on?"

"Uh-huh."

She waves one hand. "Now pick it up and pan around for a little bit, so I've got some film to work with."

The camera has a little foldout window on the side that shows me what I'm shooting, so I don't always have to use the viewfinder. I walk over to a coffee table and pan Marcie's collection of little carvings: lizards, birds, snakes, and a few hearts made out of amber and jade. When I get to Colleen she, of course, gives me the finger.

When Marcie signals, I turn the camera off and follow her back to her desk, where she mutters about firewire ports and iLinks, taps her keyboard a couple of times, and shows my movie.

"Gee, it's shaky, isn't it?"

"Uh-huh. It doesn't have any built-in stabilization. You might have to get a tripod, especially if you want to use the zoom."

I look down at my left side. "Nobody's gonna want to talk to me."

Marcie says she thinks they'll perk right up in front of a camera. "It's *The Real World* to them. It's *Survivor*. They're the digital generation."

"And if they don't," Colleen adds, "they'll find themselves driving down to Main Street to get their, uh, school supplies."

"But what do I ask them?"

"Start with the obvious. Do they like high school."

"Marcie, who's going to say they like high school?"

"Do you?"

"No. Well, wait a minute." I glance at Colleen. "Lately it's been a little better."

"See, now I want to know why. And so does the guy watching your movie."

"But most kids aren't going to say that. They're going to say they're scared."

"Because . . ."

"Does the word *guns* ring a bell?" Colleen says.

"A trick our teacher shared with us is to just ask questions that you'd like to have answered."

"Actually, I'd like to know what it's like to be a tough guy."

Colleen says she knows who'd answer that one in a hot minute, and that makes me remember Ed, something I don't like to do.

Marcie starts to fiddle with the camera. "And you can't be the only one who wants to know things like that. So you talk to enough kids and you hope they're honest with you. Then a little editing, and you're home free." She leans over her blue iMac and taps a key. "Now watch this."

Up comes a kind of control panel: a grid with eight slide-sized compartments, a bar at the bottom, and an empty screen.

A few more taps and mouse adjustments and on that shelf on the right are some stills — my feet, Marcie's smiling face, her glass-enclosed knickknacks.

"This is the movie essentially. If you hit Play now, it'll roll out just the way you shot it. But if you want my face to go before your feet, here's all you do. Just drag it down to this time line" — She points to the bar across the bottom of the screen — "and it's done. Now when you show the film, I'm first. If you want that coffee table first, drag it down. Couldn't be simpler."

"So if I interview ten kids, I can put anybody I want in any order?"

"For maximum effect. Exactly."

At the door Marcie hugs us both good night. Colleen and I start down the walk. I clutch the camera and some extra film.

"That was pretty cool."

Colleen lights a Marlboro. "It was all right. I got a little tired of being cordial. Let's go dancing."

"Are you kidding?"

"No. Let's go to the Aorta Club. Anybody who hasn't been to the Aorta is wasting his life. I know that because it's full of Buddhists. Dancing Buddhists."

"Colleen, I can't dance."

"Bullshit. I'll teach you."

"No, I mean one leg is shorter than the other."

"Everybody dances like that at the Aorta. You'll fit right in."

I glance across the street at the still-dark house. And the locked garage. "Grandma doesn't . . ." I stop.

"Grandma doesn't what, Bancroft?"

I hang my head. "Doesn't let me stay out on a school night."

Colleen points. "If you don't put that cerebral-palsied ass of yours in my car right now, I am never speaking to you again."

"I better at least leave her a note." I lead the way to the front porch, then dig in my pocket. "In case she wakes up."

"How did I know," Colleen says, coming up behind me, "that you'd have a little gold pencil and a notepad."

"Grandma gave 'em to me." I'm trying to write. "Leave me alone."

She puts both arms around my waist. "No way. Guys with little gold pencils get me hot."

I take as long as I can to slip the piece of paper under the door because I know Colleen is just goofing around, but I like the feel of her arms around me, anyway. I'm also thinking that this is the plan Grandma and I made: if I'm ever out late, I have to call or leave a note. We talked about it like I was a regular kid, with regular arms and legs. A kid with buddies or a girlfriend. A kid in the Drama Club. A kid with a car. And we both knew it would never happen. I'd never be late, ever. And if something at the Rialto went past ten o'clock, she waited up for me.

"Hey!" Colleen stops hugging and hits me. "Are we going or not?"

I limp to the car, where I try to open the door for her.

"That doesn't work anymore." She vaults into the ripped seat. "But yours does."

I inspect the ancient VW convertible, one of those where the top just folds down. I can see the rusted frame. Tattered pieces of canvas cling to it like the remains of sails on the *Flying Dutchman.*

"What do you do when it rains?"

"Get wet." She leans across and pushes the door open for me. I turn sideways, fall into the seat, get my left leg in first, grope for the seat belt.

"What are you thinking?" she asks. "That you're gonna go flying out and hurt yourself?"

"Very funny. Listen, how am I going to get in this place? I'm not exactly twenty-one."

"Don't worry. Number one—I know everybody. Number two—they stamp the shit out of your hand so nobody'll sell you a drink."

As she pumps on the gas pedal and swears, I look up at the big oaks that flank the street. The Santa Anas are still blowing, the same winds that tear through Raymond Chandler's novels. In the movie version of *The Big Sleep,* Martha Vickers tells Humphrey Bogart that he's not tall, and he replies, "I try to be."

When we finally get going, I will myself to relax. I'm sitting in a car; I look like anybody else.

We tear down Mission toward the freeway, past the local hardware store where the clerks know your name, past the coffee shop where somebody always sits writing in a journal. When we catch a red light at Orange Grove, a Volvo pulls up beside us. In the back sits a kid maybe twelve or thirteen. He's got his baseball hat on backward. Both ears are covered by headphones, and he's rocking out to something his parents hate.

Then he looks over and I swear to God I can read his thoughts: Oh, man. I want some chick in a thrashed ride to chauffeur my ass around someday.

I'm not cool, I say to myself, *but I try to be.*

Half an hour later we make our way up a dark street somewhere in Hollywood. Motorcycles leak oil onto a couple of patchy lawns. Every telephone post blooms with posters for bands and clubs.

I'm half-scared, half-stoked. I'm usually in bed by this time. "Do you think your car will be all right?"

"Unless there's a clever band of thieves who target old, rusted-out convertibles."

Just then two people get out of a VW van. He sports a Mohawk, unlaced boots, army fatigues; she settles for chains from her nose to both ears and a mini-shroud. As the couple angles across the street, I feel myself tense. I pin Marcie's camera to my side with my bad arm; that way the thief will be too disgusted to steal it.

Then the guy waves. "Hey, Colleen!"

"Hey, Ricky."

We stop and let them intercept us.

"Where's Ed?"

"Who knows."

Ricky looks me up and down. "Who's this?"

"Filmmaker."

"No shit! What are you doin' down here, man?"

"I, uh, you know. Scouting for locations."

"All right." He holds out his clenched

fist and, thanks to MTV, I know enough to tap it with mine. "What happened to your leg?"

Before I can answer Colleen says, "He laid his Harley down on the freeway."

Ricky grimaces. "Ouch. At least you were wearin' a helmet." Then he motions to Colleen and they drift away.

I smile at his girlfriend, who has her gravedigger's makeup on. Nothing. Out of the corner of my eye I see Colleen shake her head and shrug. I hear her say, "Sorry."

Ricky trudges toward me. "Put me in your film, man. Make me feel like I didn't get all dressed up for nothing."

I lift the camera. "Say something."

"Uh." He appeals to Miss Mortal Coil, but she's no help. Finally he waves and says, "Hi, Mom."

When they're far enough ahead so they can't hear I repeat, "'He laid his Harley down on the freeway?'"

"Why be a spaz when you can be a wounded warrior?"

"Well, there's always the truth, that quaint concept."

"You are what you say you are."

"What does Ricky say he is?"

"Ricky? He likes to be the first on his block."

"First on his block to what?"

"You name it. Some new drug: he'll take it. Some new club: he's been there. He'll, like, drive to San Diego to hear a band that might turn out to be the new Hole or some guy who might be the next Gavin Rossdale. He likes to be able to say, 'Oh, yeah. I saw him at Jugular when he was just starting.'"

"What about her?"

"Cindy? She's with Ricky."

We turn down an alley that's a gauntlet of people smoking cigarettes. I feel their eyes on me. On my bad leg. And on my camera. Colleen nods to some black guys, and I slow down to watch a couple of riot girls giggling and wrapping their wallet chains around each other's wrists.

"Hey," one says, "what's up?"

Colleen waves them away. "Not tonight."

I read the names on the posters: Skanic, Wet, Polar Goldie Cats, Cea Jacuzzi. I like the bright colors and the way new posters have been half stripped away so the old ones underneath show. I raise the camera and run off a few yards of film.

Colleen comes back for me and hustles us past a little line and right up to the guy at the door, who stands underneath a tiny neon sign: AORTA.

"Hey, Viper," Colleen says. "What's shakin'?"

Viper peers at me through his dreadlocks. "Who's he?"

"He's making a movie."

"What happened to you, man?"

Colleen answers for me. "Fell when he was rock climbing up at Joshua Tree."

Viper grimaces as he steps aside to let us in.

As I hobble down the stairs, I say, "As reckless as I am, it's a wonder I can walk at all."

Colleen spreads her arms like a ringmaster. "Don't tell your grandma, but you are as of right now a certified clubgoer."

Aorta has three rooms—three chambers, I guess, like an imperfect heart. Behind door number one is a small room with a makeshift bar and old drywall stacked in one corner. There are a couple of amps in the corner of room number two, but the crowd is in the back listening to a band named Clinical Trials.

All the guys on the rickety stage either have their shirts off or they wear thrashed tank tops. Their skin glows white. The lead singer mutters the lyrics ominously, like a postal worker with an Uzi in his gym bag.

"If this was an old cowboy movie," I say, "I'd lurch over to the bar, order a sarsaparilla, and the whole place would get real quiet."

"You'd better pee instead."

"What kind of cowboy movies have you been watching?"

"Before it gets totally crowded, smart-ass." She points. "You're this way, I'm that way. Meet you in a minute."

I get into a short line leading into the men's room. The three other guys leaning against the wall look like Indolence, Idleness, and Sloth. Guitar players trickle in through some invisible back door, clutching their instruments like enormous rare artifacts. On the wall across from me someone has scrawled: *Its not How high are you? Its Hi how are you?*

I watch a girl in a gold tube top dial the only phone. She puts one finger in her ear and frowns as she listens. "I'm as committed as you," she bellows. "I am, too. I just can't come home right now. I've gotta hear this band." Marcie would like her; she was pretty clearly passionate about something.

My camera gets a lot of attention in the bathroom. In fact, it just about clears the place. Then two guys in leather pants have a little argument that explains everything:

"He can't be a narc, man. Look at him."

"The perfect cover, if you ask me."

"Are you a narc, man?" asks Leather Pants 1.

I shake my head. "Gee, no."

Leather Pants 2 sneers, "What's he gonna say, man?"

They eye each other. Then me. Then they bolt. Or split, as the locals would probably say. Split at top speed.

When I find Colleen a minute or so later she bows politely. "May I have this—"

"I really don't dance, okay?"

"You just need a little E."

"You sound like Vanna White."

"You watch *Wheel of Fortune?*"

"Grandma does. But she doesn't know that I know. It's one of those guilty pleasures."

"Ed's mom loves that show. Sometimes we watch it with her." I let her lead me into the center of the floor. "Ed's pathetic. The board will have something like The o-u-n-d of Music. And he'll look at me and say, 'Hound?' 'Pound?'"

"In 'The Hound of Music' this big dog from the Baskerville estate kills Julie Andrews. It's on my top-ten list."

"Shut up and dance."

So I try, but I'm totally self-conscious.

"How am I doing?" I ask.

"Let's put it this way: you're making everybody else look a whole lot better." She takes hold of my belt loops. "Move your hips."

"Ask them to play 'The Monster Mash.'"

"Very funny." Colleen puts her warm palm over my mouth. But gently. "And let's get rid of that camera. Keep an eye on me."

I watch her scamper to the bar and hand the camera to a guy with huge biceps and one of those sinister goatees. When she points at me, I wave, and he gives me the thumbs-up sign.

All of a sudden, the bass player smashes his guitar in what I guess is an angst-ridden fit. Some people keep on dancing to the music in their heads. Most of us stop, but nobody leaves the floor—not that there's anywhere to sit, anyway.

Just then a guy with a lot of metal in his face sidles up to Colleen and whispers something.

She shakes her head. "Not tonight."

"C'mon," he says, "I've got the money."

"I don't care if you've got an American Express card. I don't have anything."

"Don't be a bitch."

"Fuck you, Vincent. Take a hike."

When he just stands there, I step closer. "You heard her. Why don't you mosey along?"

He glares down at me but asks Colleen, "Where's Ed? What are you doing with this loser?"

Colleen takes hold of my shirt and pulls me into the crowd. "Are you nuts? 'Why don't you mosey along?'"

"I always wanted to say that to somebody. I've heard it in about a million Westerns."

"Well, I can take care of myself, sheriff. You don't want to mess with Vincent. He's mean."

I take both of her hands. "What *are* you doing with me?"

"Don't get all serious on me, Ben. I'm having a good time."

"I'm not getting all serious. I'm just curious."

"I'm here, okay? And you're here. We're dancing. I'm not doing anything with you except dancing."

"But you like me."

Colleen takes a deep breath. "Not in the way you mean."

"What way, then?"

"You'll get mad if I tell you."

"No, I won't."

"Guys always say that. Then they get mad."

"I won't. I promise."

Colleen glances around. She puts both hands on my shoulders. She leans into me. I like this. If I'm going to get bad news, this is the way to get it. "When I'm with Ed," she says, "sometimes I end up in a little room in Watts where all the guys have got guns and all the girls hate me because I'm white.

"But you want to make a movie, you're worried about getting into college, you like to kiss. When I'm with you, it's like I'm really in high school."

She steps back then. The band plays a few long, ugly chords. The dance floor starts to fill up again.

"I'm not mad."

"Really?"

"Colleen, it's true. I *am* in high school. So are you."

"So we're still dancing?"

"Sure." Because I'm not going to think about what she said as much as I'm going to think about her leaning into me while she said it.

So I try dancing again, and I'm actually doing better, actually looking less like somebody with one foot nailed to the floor, when a bare-chested dervish whirls by and I take an elbow to the cheek. I go right down right on my butt.

"Man!" I feel my face. "What was that all about?"

"Some fucking mosher." Colleen crouches beside me. People peer down at me. "C'mon. Get up. I see him."

"I'm okay. It's no big deal."

"It's not okay. Get up and deck that fucker." She holds out one hand and helps me to my feet.

"I've never decked anybody in my life."

"Then it's about time."

"Easy for you to say. If things don't work out, you can actually flee. I, on the other hand, have a tragic wound from trying to rock climb on my Harley."

"He lays one fucking finger on you, I'll put the hurt on him in a big way."

There's a great word to describe Colleen's eyes right that second: coruscating. Emitting vivid flashes of light. She emits a few more, then leans into me. And kisses me. "Now let's go."

But we don't get anywhere near the guy who'd hit me, because Ed slithers out of the dark and right up to Colleen.

"Hey, I went by your place."

Colleen sticks out her tongue at him, like a seven-year-old. Then she dances away, putting a guy in leather pants between them.

Ed follows her. I follow Ed. We weave through the crowd.

"I have got some shit you will not believe, Colleen. It's like one-toke hash but better. Unbelievably smooth. No paranoia, no nothing. It's gorgeous. You're gonna love it."

Colleen slips between two girls, one in red, the other in green. Like stoplights.

When Ed turns around and frowns, there I am. He looks me up and down, then asks Colleen, "What's goin' on here?"

"Leave Ben alone. He just asked me to show him around. And why not, huh? You were busy with Ms. Wonderbra."

"Hey, she was buying a ton of product for a kegger."

"You took her out for lunch."

Ed tucks his hands under both biceps so they look big enough to write an essay on. "To seal the deal is all. Relax." He leans and whispers something.

Colleen shakes her head. "No, I'm dancing. With Ben."

"Bring him along." Ed glances down at me. "You want to party with us? This is very good stuff. If you like it, you know where to get more."

"I mean it, Ed. Leave him alone."

"Let him decide for himself. Hey Ben, you want to party or not?"

Colleen won't look right at me anymore. "Don't let him talk you into anything, Ben."

I watch Ed put one arm around her. I watch her pretend to struggle, then lean into him. I say, "You came with me."

She kisses Ed. On the lips. "Give me a second here, baby." But she's talking to him. Of course.

When she looms over me, I feel like I'm about to be taken to the principal.

"Look, Ben, this was a field trip, okay? What did you think—that I was gonna be your girlfriend? You're a sweet kid, but you were just something to do until Ed showed up."

AS I PROWL THE HALLS the next morning, I catch people looking at me, checking out my bruises and cuts. Guys eye me; girls glance, whisper to each another, and glance again.

Then I round a corner and there's Colleen propped against the wall outside her homeroom. I stalk right up to her, and I mean it this time. Bad leg or no bad leg, I stalk.

"Boy, that was really crappy."

She barely opens her eyes.

"What happened to your face?"

"Remember that guy who knocked me down? I found him and tried to knock him down. You can see how that turned out."

"How did you get home?"

"I took a cab."

"I couldn't believe it when you split. We would have dropped you off."

"You came with me."

"Ben, I drove! You came with me!"

"You know what I mean. What you did was really crappy."

Colleen just fumbles for her sunglasses and puts them on. "Lookit, I wasn't going to use last night, all right? Before I left for Marcie's, I did what you said and left my stash at home." She pulls up her Ramones T-shirt and wipes at her nose. "But I go to the bathroom at the club and this girl I know has got some coke. And then I run into this other chick who's got some dolphins. You know when we were dancing and having a good time? I was high. That scene with Marcie made me nervous; I couldn't wait to get high. Then Ed shows up with this shit and he's not kidding: it's the best I ever smoked."

I take off my book bag, something Ed would never carry, something none of the cool guys ever carry. "You don't have to keep doing it, though."

Colleen digs in her purse for a Kleenex. "Remember when Marcie asked us what kids were passionate about? Well, I like drugs. I'm passionate about drugs."

I shake my head. "Not all the time. You could be like those Buddhist guys—you fall down, you get up."

"No, I like falling down too much." She looks at the ground. She's wearing shower clogs, thick blue ones. Her feet are long and white.

"Colleen, listen—"

"You listen. We're history, okay?" She's so loud people stop to stare.

"I don't want to be history." I'm as loud as she is. "Anyway, you're just hung-over. You'll feel different tomorrow. You know you will."

"Yeah? Well, if I do, I'll just smoke another joint. Make your little movie, Ben. Forget about me."

I watch her turn and walk away. Her pants are dirty. The tag on her precious Fresh Jive T-shirt sticks up. She's wearing those stupid shoes. I bellow, "Fine. I will. And it's not little, either!"

ARTIE WEBSTER FOLLOWS ME into an empty classroom. I motion for him to sit behind the teacher's desk, then plant myself in front of him. I look through the viewfinder.

"I'm going to ask you some questions, okay?" When he doesn't answer I glance up. "Okay?"

"Yeah, sure. I was just thinking your voice is different than I remember. Higher. More like a girl's."

"Very funny."

"When's the last time you talked to any-body?"

"I talk in class."

"That doesn't count."

"Well, I'm talking now. So will you answer some questions? I'm making a movie."

"What about?"

"High school."

"Any girls in it? Like, at the beach? Or unconscious?"

"Try and relax, Artie."

"What happened to your face?"

"Hey, who's interviewing who here?"

"You ask me one, I'll ask you one. I go first—what happened to your face?"

"I got in a fight."

"Somebody hit you? That was chicken shit."

"Maybe I'm tougher than I look."

"Man, you better be."

"My turn to ask a question: What do you want out of high school?"

Artie pretends to think. "All right. What I want out of high school is to prepare myself for the future in the best way possible."

I roll my eyes. "Scene one, take two."

"To get out of this place alive, then, okay? That's my biggest goal."

"That's more like it. And then what?"

"Are you kidding? Go to college."

"So you feel like high school prepared you for college?"

"Hey, my dad says you get out of things what you put into them."

"But what do you say?"

"I just told you."

I look over the top of the camera. "No, no. I mean what do *you* believe?"

"Huh?"

I glance at my list of questions, a list Colleen and I thought up together. "Forget it. If you could change one thing about high school, what would it be?"

"Do you know Stephanie Brewer?"

"Jeremy's girlfriend?"

"That's the change I'd make. There'd be more girls like Stephanie."

"So there'd still be metal detectors and gangs and burned-out teachers but way more Stephanies?"

Artie leans forward. "But there wouldn't be gangs then, so we wouldn't need metal detectors."

"Why not?"

"Stephanie jerks Jeremy off."

"So?"

"So if everybody had a Stephanie, everybody'd be happy."

"Can I quote you? I need one more source for my term paper on Utopia."

"Hey, you should know what I'm talking about. You had Colleen."

"I never had Colleen."

"You can tell me, man."

"Artie, I know where this is going, so just don't, okay?"

"But I heard that Ed said when Colleen was high she'd do any—"

I loom over the desk and put my bruised face right in Artie's. "Shut up, man. I'm not kidding."

Stephanie Brewer leans against the north wall of the gym, the wall with the big panther logo.

"Move a little to the left, okay?"

"Who else is in this movie?" she asks.

"So far just you and Artie."

"Who's Artie?"

"A little more to the left." I look through the viewfinder. "I kind of want that panther's paw to show up in the frame."

"Did Ed do that to your face?"

"No."

"Well, it looks kinda cute."

"Yeah, right."

"Well, it's not bad. What's bad is those clothes your grandma makes you wear. And how you think you're better than everybody else."

"I never thought that."

"It sure looked like it. Two years ago I asked you to run for treasurer of the freshman class, and all you did was glare at me."

"You just felt sorry for me."

"I needed a treasurer, and you're good at math."

I raise the camera. With her blue pedal pushers and banana-colored top she could have stepped right out of an ad. "Ready?"

"Do you want me to do anything special?"

"Just answer the questions." I glance at my list. "Do you feel safe at school?"

Stephanie frowns. "Most of the time. High school's kind of like L.A.: you're fine if you know what you're doing. And like they say— there's safety in numbers."

"Meaning?"

"You know who my friends are."

"The jocks."

"Exactly. Even the really bad kids go to the games. And they know who's with who. So I don't get hassled very much."

"You mean guys like Spoonhead care if we beat Compton or not?"

"For sure. But like summers are kind of

119

bad, because there's no games and people get high and forget and stuff. And after graduation is really bad because then you're just another white face. But Shaunelle and Lourdes really helped. They told me what to do."

"Meaning what, exactly?"

"Like when some blunted-out homie starts in on me, I get right in his face. I give him back twice as bad. You can't ever let them know you're scared. I learned more from those two girls than I ever learned in classes. Stuff I could really use. Not like George Orwell and Virginia Woolf."

"Sounds like you're anxious to get out."

Stephanie puts both hands on her hips and tries to look saucy. "How's this?"

"Fine. Are you anxious to get out of high school?"

"It's like . . . okay, it's a jungle and all that, but it's my jungle, you know? There's animals and stuff, but they're animals I see every day. And if there's quicksand, I know where it is. College is going to be really different. Everybody says how much better it'll be not worrying about guns, but I'll bet it's way harder. I get good grades because I remember what teachers say in class and I'm no trouble. Kids come back from college all the time because they flunked out."

"But at least you'll be with Jeremy."

"Jeremy will last maybe half a semester. He thinks he can play college ball, but all he can really do is stand in one spot and hit three-pointers. He's not all that tall and he gets intimidated anywhere inside the paint."

"Man, that's cold."

"I'm just realistic, Ben." As I fiddle with the camera, she meanders toward me. "Speaking of which: What was it with you and Colleen? I mean, was that realistic?"

"Obviously not."

"She's kind of a lowlife, anyway. You're better off without her."

"Take that back."

Stephanie frowns at me. "What?"

"Take back what you said."

"You think she's not a lowlife? Are you kidding?"

"I don't listen to people badmouth Colleen."

Stephanie shrugs. "Fine. I take it back. Jesus, what's got into you?"

I sit at a table near the back of the cafeteria, talking to three girls. Each one's got her head cocked at a different angle. Two have their arms crossed.

"You think we don't know who you are?" says a girl named Chana. "Your grandma's the one shows up at the park every Thanksgiving wearing those little plastic gloves and handin' out food to the darkies."

"You know my grandma?"

Debra snorts. "One eye on that big-assed Cadillac of hers, the other up to Heaven where God's got nothin' else to do but put gold stars right next to her name."

I nod. "Sounds like her. But she's not here. I am."

"Why are you askin' us last?"

I just look at her. "You're not last."

"Really. Well, Jeremy said no, and Spoonhead said no and a lot of other people said no."

I pick up my camera. "Sorry I bothered you."

Molly pulls her blue-and-white Adidas jacket around her. "Wait a minute. What all do you want to know?"

It's too hard to get all the way up. I lean on the table. "About stuff you've been through. I mean, you all are seniors with babies and you always sit over here by yourselves. What's that like?"

Debra leans forward. "I'll tell you what you should be doin' with your time, and that's makin' a movie about birth control. You do that and you can put my big ass right in the middle of the picture." She leans toward the camera. "You don't want to end up like me, stay out the back seat of the car, don't go in nobody's room to look at no NBA highlights, and keep a lock on your panties twenty-four seven."

"Do you still see the fathers of your children?"

Molly shrugs. "Around. I see mine around, carrying his basketball instead of his baby."

"So do you go out on dates and stuff?"

The three girls look at each other. "Well, it's hard," Chana says finally. "When my grandma can't baby-sit, I can't go anywhere. And she'll only baby-sit so much, so it's either go to school or go dancing. And without school, I'm in more trouble than I am now."

"I'm just not interested," Debra says.

Molly blushes. "I'm interested, but all guys want is to do the nasty. They think 'cause I did it at least once I'm just gonna fall on the nearest bed."

"What do you want to do after you graduate?"

Chana grins. "I want to sit on the beach and have people give me money. But that position has apparently already been filled 'cause I never see it up on the Job Board."

"My sister started at Macy's part-time. Now she's an assistant buyer. I could do that."

Molly says, "My people make soap and go to craft fairs. Lot of single mothers in that business."

Chana glances down. "Oh, man. I'm leakin' again." She turns to me, and I angle the Sony. "What's wrong with this picture? You're not supposed to leak milk on your Gap T-shirt. You wear a Gap T-shirt, you're supposed to be dancin' at a cookout and bein' all happy 'cause you're more comfortable than anybody in the world." Chana puts her hand over the lens. "Do I get to ask you a question now?"

I turn off the camera. "Sure."

"What's the story with you and Colleen?"

I stand up. "Thanks for talking to me."

Chana scowls. "Oh, fine. Get all cold on me now. You're crippled, little man, not blind. Are you telling me you couldn't see the two of you got nothin' whatsoever in common?"

MY GRANDMOTHER GETS UP EARLY, but since she does yoga and checks to see what the stock market is doing, we don't always bump into each other. But all of a sudden there she is, looking like an icicle in white linen slacks and a white blouse. She sits across from me as I stare blearily at my cereal.

"You remind me so much of your grandfather, Benjamin. He'd brood and stay up late, too. It was best to let him alone. Sooner or later, he'd be his old self."

"I've just been across the street, Grandma. Working on that project I told you about."

"I know there's something on your mind besides a home movie. If talking about it would make you feel the least bit better, I'm available."

"Grandma, it's not gonna do any good. And, anyway, you don't want to hear it."

"Because it's about that girl."

I look up from the last of my Cheerios, each one like the empty life preserver of a doomed ship. "She's got a name."

She reaches for the faded bruise on my cheek. "Did the boyfriend do this?"

"No. This isn't a Sean Penn movie, Grandma."

"But she prefers him."

"Colleen likes drugs. And her boyfriend's got a lot of those."

She nods. "What is it exactly that you see in her? Besides the narcotics, she's so profane and . . ." She thinks for a few seconds. "So badly decorated."

I reach for her hand. "Grandma, you're really a hoot."

She picks at the cuff of my seventy-dollar shirt, the one that she sends to the best laundry in town. "Some men like to rescue women. I hope you're not one of those."

"Grandma, in the last three years, except for you, she's the only person who actually touched me, actually put her hands on me." I shake my stunted arm at her. "She touched this, she touched my stupid leg. It was like it didn't matter. When I was with her sometimes I felt like John Travolta in *Saturday Night Fever* bopping down the street carrying that can of paint.

"And we had fun. We talked on the phone, we went to Marcie's movie, we went to a club. And I know you don't like her, Grandma, but when she's with me, I swear to God, she's different, too. And I just know that if I wasn't like I am . . ."

And then I cry. I can't help it. Grandma waits, then hands me one of her perfect little linen handkerchiefs.

I blow my nose. "Sorry. I just—"

"Benjamin, I don't know what you see in that girl. But I do know this: everybody, and I mean everybody, stands in front of the mirror and wishes they were different."

AT SCHOOL, I DODGE SOME JOCKS with their arms around each other's shoulders, cut between a couple holding hands, and pull up beside Oliver Atkins.

"Oliver, can I talk to you a minute?"

"So, Benjamin, what shall we begin with: my impeccable taste in clothes or those show tunes I can't help but hum?"

"So you already know about the documentary?"

"Oh, sure. But the real buzz is about you."

"What about me?"

"Are you kidding? You're like this high school Lazarus."

All of a sudden I'm honest-to-God dizzy thinking about wasting years of my life, years of this incarnation. I have to bite down hard to keep my jaw from quivering. I raise my camera. "Can we, uh, just do this, please?"

"I'm ready when you are. Shall we step outside?"

"No, no. Let's just let people stream by behind you."

"You're the director, Mr. Scorsese."

I look at the questions on my list. "Let's just start with how safe you feel around here."

"As a homosexual or as a Homo sapiens?"

"Either. Both."

"Well, as a gay man, I feel reasonably safe. I've been out since sixth grade." He raises his left arm festooned with silver bracelets. "Nobody's surprised when they see all these ornaments, for example. The teachers accept me, either because they're truly tolerant and enlightened or because they think they should be. The jocks are tired of making fun of me and to the gangstas I'm just beneath contempt. Except for school, I live in an all-gay world. My dentist is gay, my doctor is gay. I patronize a gay dope dealer."

"Do you ever stand in front of a mirror and wish you were different?"

"Only every day."

"Do you want to be not gay?"

"No. I want to be better-looking."

Stephanie's boyfriend, Jeremy, looms into the frame. "You tell 'em, faggot. You got all the answers." Then he staggers away laughing.

Oliver sighs. "Wouldn't it be nice if high school were either voc ed or college prep? That way when somebody read a poem all the boys in the back row wouldn't have to act like they're throwing up; they'd be somewhere else learning how to fix a toilet."

"What are you going to do after high school?"

"Probably move to San Francisco. My parents hate me."

"You said probably. If you don't do that, what else would you like to do?"

"Join the navy. Now can I ask you a question?"

I turn off the camera. "I guess."

"Are you gay?"

"Are you kidding?"

"Let's start with the way you do neat-and-clean. Add that look-but-don't-touch act of yours to a fag hag grandma and I'm thinking you might be deeper in the closet than my poly-ester flares."

"I'm not gay."

"So Colleen wasn't just a beard. You really liked her?"

"Yeah."

"But she's back with Ed."

I nod.

"If you're so butch, get her back."

"Oh, sure."

"Hey, you're the cinephile: meet him in the middle of some dusty street at high noon."

I go right to the parking lot where Ed tends to hang out. Is Oliver making me do it? I don't know. But I have to do something.

Sure enough, there's Ed by his spotless Camaro. He leans on the fender. Everybody else keeps a respectful distance from the paint job. Four or five guys and a couple of girls listen to him, then laugh on cue. When he spots me, he stops his monologue.

"What's up, spaz?" The studs in his eyebrow ascend, registering the question.

I glance at Colleen, who's slumped in the front seat sipping gingerly at a can of 7UP. I'm glad to see her, but she doesn't look too good.

"I was worried about her."

Ed points to the car. "Somebody should be. She could be in one of those movies you like so much, you know? *Invasion of the Zombies* or something." Ed's T-shirt is tight, but he inhales, anyway, so I can see the slabs of his pectoral muscles.

"How do you know what kind of movies I like?"

"Are you kidding? When she gets loaded, you're all she talks about, and she's loaded most of the time."

I go over to the car, open the door. "Want to take a little walk?" I hold out my good hand.

Colleen takes it blindly and gets out one limb at a time: first a leg, then one arm, the other leg. When she finally finds her purse, she clutches it like a courier carrying news that could alter the course of the war.

Ed sidles up to me. "Just for the record: I'm giving her to you, you're not taking her away from me."

I watch a girl named Heather step up beside him. She slips one thumb into his belt loop. She's got big boobs and she presses one of them into Ed's arm. She's been waiting for this. She's the understudy and this is her big chance.

I take Colleen by the arm to steady her. "You okay?"

She swallows hard. "I don't think so."

Behind me, somebody says something, somebody else laughs at me. Or Colleen. And I want to turn around and shut him up. I want to hurl myself at him. God help me, I want a gun. Man, I have seen way too many movies.

I ask Colleen, "What do you want to do?"

"I don't know."

"I'll take you home."

"Fuck, no."

"We can go to my house."

"And have your grandma croak? No way."

"You should eat."

"Like I could keep it down. Give me your hand. I'm all, like, woozy and shit."

We haven't gone ten yards before Colleen stops. She puts both hands to her face. "I'm all fucked up, Ben."

"It'll wear off."

"No, not just the weed. More like everything."

I point. "Your car's just over here. Can you drive?"

Colleen shakes her head.

"Then we'll take the bus."

"No, I'm sick, Ben. I'm really sick."

COLLEEN DOESN'T WANT ME to see her in the hospital. "I look like shit" pretty much explains why. After about a week, though, she knows when she's getting out, so I block off those days on my calendar, then cross them out one by one like some guy in prison.

She calls me every day, sometimes twice, and usually after school when I'm at Marcie's working on *High School Confidential,* which is what I've decided to call my movie. I stop whatever I'm doing to talk to her. I roam the house, looking out the window at Marcie on her knees in the flower bed.

I want to tell Colleen I love her, but I don't. I don't even say I miss her, because she doesn't say she misses me. She talks a lot about the other people in her ward—one of them's a child actor I've heard of—and about the crappy food. She does say one of the first things she wants to do when she gets out is go to the Rialto, so that's a good sign.

We agree to meet in front of the theater. Right after her meeting.

I get there first. Big surprise. I don't pace—people with C.P. find other ways to be nervous—but I could pace. I'm worried about Colleen, so I'm glad to see her crappy little car cruise by, glad to see her wave and point to a parking spot. I do my best to amble that way.

"Hey!" She clambers out, grabs her purse out of the back, and kisses me.

"I missed you." I can't help myself.

"Me, too. I told my group about you. I said you were the cleanest, soberest guy in the world. Half the chicks in there want to be your girlfriend."

I put my arm around her. If possible, she's skinnier than before. "How was your meeting?"

"Well, I asked God to remove all character defects and shortcomings, and He said He'd have to get back to me on that because there are only so many hours in a day."

She's wearing pedal pushers, white sneakers, and a T-shirt without a band's name on it.

"You look good."

"I feel pretty good. I'm taking my vitamins." She kisses me again, fast and hard. "How's your movie?"

"Done, I think." I hold up my crossed fingers. "I just need to show it to Marcie."

"Have you got my assignments? Did my teachers, like, freak?"

"They were okay. I just said you were sick."

When she digs in her purse, I flinch. She says, "Relax. I'm just going to smoke a cigarette." Then she frowns at the little flip-top box in her hand. "Wait a minute. I just smoked about a hundred of these things. Let's go in. And don't let me have any Coke, either. With a capital *C*, I mean."

I point to the marquee, which says APOCA-LYPSE NOW. "This is a really good movie."

"You should know, baby."

Baby. Stuff like that gives me such a rush. Every now and then Grandma calls me *dear,* but that just makes me feel like Bambi.

When we get in the short line, Colleen leans against me. Under her new clothes, I can feel every inch of her long, thin body.

"I was reading this brochure before the meeting?"

"Yeah?"

"There's a twelve-step program for everything," she says. "Ever hear of Debt Anon? Cross-Dressers Anon?"

"You're kidding."

"No way. 'Hello, I'm Carl, and I'm wearing Donna Karan.'"

I step up to Mrs. Stenzgarden, put down a twenty-dollar bill, and say, "Two, please." Then I just look at the tickets.

And keep looking at them as we make our way up the little incline and across the turquoise-and-black tiles.

"I never bought two tickets before. It feels weird."

"Poor baby. You should have gone to All by Myself Anon."

I introduce Colleen to Reginald and tell him this is kind of an anniversary: six weeks ago to the day, Colleen and I met at the Rialto.

He gallantly kisses her hand and says that in honor of the occasion the snacks are on the house.

At the concession stand, Colleen peers through the smeared glass. "We need to get a lot of disgusting stuff," she says. So we do: licorice whips, Jujubes, Milk Duds, popcorn, and Mountain Dew.

When *Apocalypse Now* starts, we sit back and eat. But pretty soon Colleen shakes her head when I offer more Milk Duds or popcorn.

The deeper Martin Sheen gets into the jungle, the closer he gets to Colonel Kurtz, the harder she holds my hand. She falls right into the movie, and I go with her. I forget about camera angles, tracking shots, and close-ups. I let the movie have me, too. We watch everything. Eventually, we surface through the names of carpenters, gaffers, drivers, and caterers.

When the lights come up Colleen's dabbing at her eyes with a Kleenex. "That was so fucking good."

I'm not quite sure what to do; I've never seen her cry before. I put my arm around her and she leans into me.

"And you know what?" she says. "I'll bet that's the first movie I've seen all the way through since I was, like, ten. I was always loaded. I fucking slept through half my fucking life. Fuck!" She sits up straight and blows her nose. "How long is this here for?"

I shrug. "A week, probably."

"Let's see it again. Do you want to see it again?"

"I'll have to ask my grandma." I say it like a real weenie. On purpose. And then I kind of scrunch up and protect myself because I know Colleen is going to beat on me, and Colleen plays rough.

MARCIE LEANS FORWARD and puts her right arm around my shoulders. "I talked to my teacher, and he called the guy who runs the Centrist Gallery. He does this student-video thing every November, and we can send him yours as soon as you're done."

I point at the iMac. "Better check this out before we start talking about the Academy Awards."

"True." Marcie taps the keyboard and up comes *High School Confidential*. Nobody's seen it but me, not even Colleen, so I'm nervous. I sit up straighter in my bright-yellow wooden chair. I wipe my good hand on my jeans.

Twenty minutes later Marcie frowns and scratches her head.

"That bad?" I try to sound like it doesn't matter very much.

"Well, there are good parts. That line from Chana about leaking milk onto her Gap T-shirt is pure gold."

"But . . . ?"

"They're a little predictable." She massages the bridge of her nose. "The gay guy is gay. The black girls are black. If I want to see stereotypes, I'll watch television."

"But Oliver *is* gay, and he makes sure everybody knows it. If Chana, Molly, and Debra aren't together, they're with some other black kid."

"Talk to them."

"Marcie, I did talk to them."

"No, you interviewed them. Talk to them this time."

"And then what?" I point at the screen. "Do I have to throw all this stuff away?"

"Maybe not. Maybe you can start with them defined by race and sexual preference and move deeper. You're not going to know until you really talk to them."

She stands up and I follow her to the front door. Marcie opens her purse, fishes around for a few seconds, and hands me a set of keys. "You know what to do."

"Sure." But now I don't want to do it. "Pick up the mail, water the plants, feed the fish." I try not to sound snotty.

"Ben, unless it comes up, don't tell your grandma I'm out of town. I'm not completely comfortable with the idea of you and Colleen here by yourselves."

"Why? We're not going to do anything."

"That's what I'm afraid of. The movie needs work, and you haven't got a lot of time." Marcie's wearing cargo pants and there's actually stuff in every pocket. She reaches into one. "Have you got condoms?"

At first I think she says tom-toms. Either way, the answer is no.

"Take some. You're going to be all alone with your girlfriend."

"Colleen hasn't got a disease."

"I never said she did, but nobody should sleep with anybody without some kind of protection." She acts like a pushy caterer who wants somebody to try the Special Cracker. So I choose one.

"Take two. You're sixteen." She grins, but it's fake.

She puts the rest of the condoms back in her pocket, then takes my entire face in both hands. "Promise me you'll get some work done."

I pull away. "Jesus. All right."

"Do you know you swear more than you used to?"

"Marcie, you're not my mom."

She stares down at her boots, Timberlands, actually, with red laces. "Well, somebody should be. You got short-changed in the mom department."

She turns away and fiddles with a leather overnight bag. I try to remember the last time my real mom hugged me or got on my case or talked to me about anything. I can't even remember the last thing she said to me before she evaporated.

"Marcie, I'll work hard, I really will. I'll get on the computer, go through and save just the good stuff, and then I'll talk to everybody some more."

She squeezes my good hand. "Fine. What's there is not bad, Ben, it's just . . . predictable."

"And you would know with your B minus."

I'm kidding, but she gets super-serious on me. "Ben, I didn't work hard enough. I had a boyfriend, okay? Now he's gone and I've got a stupid B minus. Don't be me. Let's get you in that gallery show. I want to get dressed up and go into Hollywood."

Just then the doorbell rings. I open the door for Colleen, who kisses me on the cheek. I try not to be obvious, but I sneak a look at her eyes. She's a little amped but probably it's just caffeine.

We walk Marcie to her yellow Xterra. We

watch her back out of the driveway then speed away.

"What's going on?" Colleen asks.

"Gee, I don't know," says Mr. Innocent.

"Bullshit." She holds up both hands, fingers up like lightning rods. "The air is like charged. Did you guys get into it?"

"Oh, yeah. Well, sort of, I guess. We were kind of talking about whether I had to do stuff she said. She's not, you know, my mom or anything."

"She's better than most moms."

I look at her. "Really?"

"Honey, she gives a shit about you. She's on your side. She wants good stuff to happen to you. She like paves the way." Colleen leads me up the walk. "I mean, she's loaning you her house so you won't miss one day working on the computer. My mom would never do that."

I hold the door. "Do I ever get to meet your mother?"

"Why? I fucking hate her."

Inside Colleen picks up the copies of *Moby Dick* and *The Scarlet Letter* that she's dropped on the counter.

"It's weird seeing you with books."

She stares at them. "Is that what these are?"

"Are you going to study?"

"I guess. God knows I should. I'm like six hundred years behind."

"Come and look at something first, okay?"

I lead her into the spare room, sit down, hit a few keys, then lean back so Colleen can see Isabel, a chubby girl with bad posture and a twenty-four-hour smirk.

"Just listen, okay? And then I want to ask you something."

Colleen sinks into the chair beside me and I hit the Play button.

"I feel," Isabel says, "like a one-woman Afterschool Special, you know? Because I've got booze everywhere: car, locker, even this little spritzer thing in my purse."

I hear myself ask, "Why?"

"It takes the edge off. It makes me feel prettier and wittier. And when shit happens, I don't take it so hard."

"You know," I say, "everybody'd tell you you're wasting the best years of your life."

"Are you kidding? I have to have a drink before I can get out of bed."

I look over at Colleen. "So here's what I want to know: does Isabel sound like a stereotype?"

"What?"

"Marcie thinks some of the kids in here are like stereotytpes."

"Isabel's a drunk. She's going to sound like a drunk."

"How do you know that?"

"I sell her a little weed every now and then. We talk."

"Why didn't she tell me?"

"Why should she trust you?"

I look up at her, kind of stunned. "God, Colleen, she admitted on camera that she's a drunk."

"That doesn't mean she trusts you. Everybody knows she's a juicer. That's old news."

I hoist myself up, one hand on the desk, one on the back of the chair. "Look at this again, then, okay? And let's see—"

All of a sudden Colleen backs away. She's all but got the crucifix and the garlic necklace. "I can't do this, Ben."

"What? Can't do what?"

She fumbles for a cigarette. "It's your movie, not mine."

"But you could help."

She shakes her head. "I helped Ed; I carried dope in my underpants."

"This is way different."

"No, I've been talking to my counselor about doing the same shit over and over. And I know this looks different, but it's not. It's the same."

Maybe an hour later I wander toward the kitchen. My shoes lie on their sides by the coffee table with its little pile of Chinese coins. Colleen sits cross-legged on the couch, frowning at a book.

"Do you want anything?" I stare into the refrigerator. "Marcie left a lot of stuff."

"I'm okay. Are you mad?"

Clutching a carrot, I sit at the other end of the couch. "No. It's okay. This is turning out to be a weird day, that's all." I glance at her. A tattooed devil stares back from her calf.

She lets *The Scarlet Letter* topple onto her thighs. "Talk about weird. It's weird being clean and sober."

"Yeah, I can imagine."

"I was looking at my tats in the mirror this morning when I got out of the shower. I feel like fucking scratch paper. I've got, like, random shit written all over me."

"Think of yourself as one of those old manuscripts with interesting stuff in the margins."

Colleen tosses the book aside and crawls toward me. "Kiss me like they did in those old movies."

"Let me put my carrot down."

The kiss lasts a long time. Then she lays her head on my chest and says, "We could fool around, you know that? There's nobody here but us."

I kiss her purple hair. "Are you sure? I don't look too good with my clothes off."

"So show me, and I'll decide. If I puke, well, then that's that."

"Can we wait till it's dark?"

"You are such a girl. What do I need—a box of chocolates and a dozen roses? Look, I'll take off my shirt, you take off your shirt."

"That's not fair. I *want* to see your . . . you know . . . with your shirt off."

"Yeah? Well, maybe I want to see your arm." She pulls up her Boy London tank top. "Tah-dah!"

I just stare.

She shrugs. "They're little."

"No. They're perfect. They're great."

"Now show me your arm."

"You have to close your eyes."

She crawls right up to me, bringing a kind of haze of cigarettes and patchouli. She smells blue. Not blue as in sad, either. Azure. That blue. "I'll help you."

The next thing I know my Ralph Lauren shirt is open. She tugs it out of my khakis, pulls the left shoulder down.

"Colleen, don't."

"Shut up. You want somebody's eyes closed, close your own."

I feel the cool air on my stomach and chest.

"Huh."

"What does that mean?"

"It means 'huh.' As in, big fucking deal."

"It's not ugly?"

"A little, but so what? Bodies are really interesting. All the shit that happens to them,

149

and they just don't quit." She takes my good hand. "C'mon."

"Where are we going?"

"Pittsburgh."

I tug at her until she stops. "Look, when we get in the bedroom, don't pay any attention to my bad side, okay? Just concentrate on the good side."

On the way I manage to get part of my shirt back on. Colleen, however, steps right out of her shorts, peels off her tank top, sits on the edge of the bed, and slips out of her underpants.

"Hey, why am I the only one with her clothes off?"

"Nobody," I say, "has ever seen me naked. I don't look at myself naked."

"Come over here, and I'll help."

I shake my head. "No way. You'll look."

"Probably."

"What if you turn your back and I undress and get into bed?"

"You're kidding."

"I know. It's like a Doris Day movie, but . . ."

"If that's what it takes, fine. We'll do it your way."

I hobble around to the other side of the bed. "This is going to take a little while."

"Should I go get *Moby Dick*?"

"Just don't look."

I struggle out of my clothes. It feels weird to just drop things on the floor. Grandma hates that. But I do it, anyway.

I ask Colleen if she's looking.

"What do you care? You've got your back to me."

"Are you under the covers?"

"No."

"Are you going to get under the covers?"

"If you are, Doris."

As quick as I can, I pull back the Navajo-print comforter. Colleen slides over beside me.

"Jesus, Ben. Your feet are freezing."

"I'm scared."

She kisses me on the forehead. "Honey, relax. The rest is easy."

I reach for my khakis, fumble in one pocket, then hold up the condom. "I've got this."

"That's cool."

"I, uh, think it takes two hands to, you know, install it."

She grabs the condom, tears the foil with her teeth, then puts it on with alarming dexterity.

"There you go," she says. "All dressed up for the party."

"What now?"

"You're kidding."

"Not totally."

"You've never seen an X-rated movie?"

"A couple."

"Well, that's how we do it."

I turn to face her. "But those people are getting paid. They might not even like each other. Isn't it different if you like the other person?"

She leans over and kisses me. "You're gonna be fine. It'll be fine."

"What's Ed like?" Boy, that jumped out by itself.

"In bed? Do you really want to know?"

"No. Yes."

She frowns like it's a hard question on a test. "Ed's relentless. And kind of industrial, you know?" She moves one arm like a piston. "Sex was never really my thing, anyway. I like getting high." She lies back. "There's one cool thing about it, though. And that's how you get to go to sleep afterward." She tugs at me. "So c'mon. Let's do it, and then we can take a little nap."

I GET INTO THE SHOW at the Centrist Gallery, which is great, but it makes me so nervous I keep fine-tuning the movie. I'm on my way to Marcie's house for the nine-thousandth time when a guy on a bicycle zips past. He's cutting in and out among the big SUVs and making everybody blow their horn.

When he shoots by me, our eyes meet. I watch him slow down, turn, and pedal back. It's Ed, riding a bike so stripped down it's nothing but a frame, wheels, and handlebars. When he slides to a stop right in front of me, I blurt, "Where's your car?"

"I totaled it."

"And you just walked away?"

He lifts his T-shirt. There's a blue-and-yellow bruise as wide as a banner. "I had my seat belt on, but Bobby didn't. He's in ICU with clamps in his head."

"Jeez, I'm sorry. I interviewed Bobby."

"For your movie, yeah. Which reminds me. Why didn't you interview me?"

"Are you kidding? I'm scared of you."

Ed likes that answer. "You live around here?"

I point across the street. "You?"

"El Serrano. Ever heard of it?"

"Sure."

"Crappy, huh." It isn't a question. "Got any brothers or sisters?"

I shake my head. "Have you?"

"Had an older brother. He was one tough son of a bitch."

"Is that where you learned?"

Ed leans on the handlebars and his triceps jump. "Probably. When it got to be winter, we'd take off all our clothes, go out in the back-yard, and see who could stand it the longest." He glances up at me. "You ever do anything like that?"

"Get serious."

"Your folks died, right? That couldn't have been easy."

Ed keeps nudging the bike forward inch by inch, moving me onto the lawn. So I push back, using my good arm to grip the handlebars, letting him run right into my bad leg. That foot is always half-turned anyway, so it makes a perfect brace. I put my knee against the knobby tire.

It's like some anti-tug-of-war, because if I lose I won't just fall back on my butt. He'll run over me.

Ed grins up at me. "I'm probably not going to graduate."

My leg is getting tired and starting to quiver from the strain. When he backs off a little, I do, too.

"What are you gonna do then?"

"My dad's so pissed about the Camaro he says I'm goin' in the army."

"I thought you were gonna be a drug kingpin and live large."

"Not many drug kingpins on bicycles." Ed

lets himself be pushed back a foot or two. "You got your pants dirty," he says.

I take my right hand off the cool metal and shake some feeling back into it. "That's okay."

Then he looks at me, squinting. "Does it hurt?"

"You mean my hand or all of it?"

"All of it."

"Sometimes."

"It hurts just to get your ass out of a chair, doesn't it?"

"It's more clumsy."

"But it never gets easier?"

"No."

"You're a tough little fucker. I couldn't handle it. I'd kill myself."

Then we just stand there. He leans on the handlebars. I put my hand in my pocket.

Then he asks, "How's Colleen? I hear she's clean and sober."

I point. "See that house? It belongs to a friend of ours. Colleen and I go over there a lot. We study and help in the garden and if we don't cook we order pizza and watch a video."

"Sounds great . . . till she shows up loaded."

156

"She won't."

"If you say so."

Then he pedals away, sitting up straight, arms out. *Look at me, Ma. No hands.*

THE NIGHT OF THE SHOW, Marcie finds a parking place just half a block from the Centrist Gallery. That means we get to walk on Melrose Avenue: tourists, panhandling kids, and a shirtless guy with his boa constrictor—five bucks to pose for a picture, his arm around Aunt Martha.

Marcie and I flank Grandma—worker bees protecting the queen. We lose Colleen in the first fifty yards, when she runs into somebody she knows. From the old days.

"Look at this!" Marcie points to the gallery window. There's my picture. And nineteen others: black guys, Hispanic girls, Chinese guys, Vietnamese girls—it's a regular UNICEF card.

I look for Colleen's leather jacket, but she's talking to a girl with blue hair.

I don't know why I'm nervous. I mean, I'm

in the show. Nobody's going to boo and throw things. If there is a review, it'll be about two inches long in one of the alternative newspapers. And they'll probably get my name wrong. Ben Boombox.

I take a big breath and let it out before I step through the door. There's a pretty good crowd. Lots of black, like a Young Morticians' Convention. Marcie stands out in her paisley overalls. In my chambray shirt and khakis, I could work for Southwest Airlines.

"You okay?" Marcie asks.

"Would you like peanuts with your in-flight beverage?"

"You look fine. C'mon, let's say hello to the guy who runs this place."

Josh turns out to be about thirty. He's wearing a pair of five-hundred-dollar pants. Grandma compliments him. He likes her Ferragamo shoes, and suddenly they're best friends.

I look for Colleen, catch her eye. She's got a glass of white wine, which she lifts in a toast. To me, I hope.

Marcie links her arm through mine and we

start at TV number one, where a big trout lectures a small one about water pollution. Marcie makes a face. "One down and nineteen to go."

We watch a few minutes of *Nihilism,* which seems to be somebody howling. But it's dark. All dark all the time. I like *Lipstick,* where a girl starts out kissing her boyfriend kind of playfully but won't stop and his face ends up completely red. And I'm crazy about *Roach Coach,* this documentary about the guys who drive those big silver snack trucks.

High School Confidential is number nine, and I think it's a good sign there's a little crowd around my TV. Actually not that little. So we decide to check out the others and then come back.

A couple are really good. Better than mine. Surer, if that makes any sense. More confident. We get something for Grandma to eat so her blood sugar won't plummet. We find her a place to sit. Then we go back to number nine.

"Is Colleen okay?" Marcie doesn't take her eyes off the screen.

"I don't know."

She grabs my arm. But nice. She's just excited. "I love this part."

"I was with some people," says Oliver. "We're at this Thai restaurant on Sunset, and a family comes in: mom, dad, and two kids, okay? A boy and a girl. A perfect family. And my friend says, 'Breeders!' loud enough for the dad to hear. And he just leaves. Turns around and takes his family with him. Everybody at the table, my table, I mean, is happy. We chased them out. We showed them.

"But I felt really shitty. Okay, I didn't say *breeders,* but I didn't not say it, either. I just sat there ashamed of myself."

Marcie grins at me.

"What?" I can't help but grin back.

She just points again.

Debra's not in the cafeteria this time, and she doesn't have her baby. We're out in the hall, down at the end where all the offices are. I can pan over to a sign saying COUNSELOR anytime I want.

"You expect a lot, Ben. You don't think I know a big word like exploitation? You're just a white boy with a camera who's lookin'

160

to do himself some good. Do you really think we're going to tell you anything that's in our hearts?" Then I fade out, and when I fade back in Debra's saying, "Molly thinks she's better than me because she's got light skin. She all the time lays her baby right by mine like we're shopping for paint and she's got the right color. Did you know she's got some Vietnamese in her somewhere? That's all she talks about. Now she wants to take a class, wants to go to Vietnam and talk to her brothers and sisters. Me, I'm all of a sudden too black for her."

Marcie sighs this big satisfied sigh, like she just had a tall glass of cool water. "How many times did you talk to her?"

"About a million."

"I am so proud of you." She turns around and hugs me.

I let her. I want her to. My C.P. doesn't matter to her. It never has. She puts her arms around all of me. So I tell her, "I couldn't have done it without you. I mean that." And I do mean it. I'm totally sincere. I just also happen to be looking for Colleen while I say it.

"What are you going to do now?" Marcie asks.

"I get the feeling that's kind of up to her."

She smiles. "I meant what's your next film project."

"Oh. Well, I've kind of been thinking about those lonely people at the Rialto." I turn to look at her. "They used to be me. Some of them still are."

Marcie nods but says, "Here comes your grandmother. I wish she wasn't so hard on Colleen."

"I know. That doesn't help."

Grandma touches my shoulder. "It seems you've caused quite a sensation. I've heard several people say that your film is one of the best things here. Congratulations, Ben."

"Thanks, Grandma."

"Film is a wonderful hobby for a young man, isn't it, Marcie?"

"It's more than a hobby, Mrs. Bancroft."

That wasn't the answer she wanted, so Grandma puts one hand to her sternum. "I know you want to celebrate, but I wonder if you'd mind dropping me at home first; it's been a tiring evening."

Marcie waves to someone. "I'll just say goodbye to a few people."

Grandma points. "And I'll be over there on that rather unforgiving couch."

I'm looking around for Colleen when somebody says, "Ben?"

A girl about my age with hair shorter and blonder than mine smiles at me. She waves the bio sheet with our digitized pictures on it. "I'm Amy. I wanted to tell you how much I liked *High School Confidential.*"

I hold out my good hand. "Not the most original title."

"No, no. It's perfect. I made *Roach Coach.*"

"Really? Oh, man, *Roach Coach* is good. How'd you get those guys who drive the trucks to open up to you?"

Amy shrugs. "I speak a little Spanish. And then I always bought something to eat and that helped. God, I gained about fifteen pounds making that film."

"No way. You look great." Then I blush.

She leans in and I smell soap and Dentyne gum. "Where are you going to film school?"

"Actually, I don't know if I am."

Amy looks genuinely concerned. "Oh, you've got to."

"Where are you going?"

"USC." She points. "It's, like, right over there. You're good enough to get a scholarship, probably, if—you know—that's the problem."

"Did you just call up and talk to somebody?"

She shakes her head. "You can do that, but it's all online."

"Oh, well. I'm not on the net. My grandma's afraid I'll watch porn."

"Oh, you've got to get hooked up. Then we could e-mail each other. I know about a thousand people who are totally into movies." She finds a piece of paper in her slacks, plucks the pen out of my chambray shirt, writes something, and hands it to me.

"For when you get e-mail." Then she backs away. "Okay? Don't forget!"

I glance around. For the first time, I've got a secret, something I don't want Colleen to see or

164

to know about. In a way, I love it. In another way, it makes me feel weirdly unfaithful.

I scan the room for her, then make my way outside. The crowd has spilled onto the sidewalk, and I look for her among the smokers.

On a hunch, I limp down toward Melrose and peek into the first alley. There she stands, up to her neck in shadows, talking to a tall guy in leather pants that creak when he moves.

"Hey, Ben. Come here, baby." She holds out the splif, but I shake my head. "Say hi to . . ."

He helps her out. "Nick."

I nod. "We're kind of going."

"Okay." She waves bye-bye to him in that woozy way people do. When we get out to the street she says, "Don't get mad, okay?"

"I didn't say anything."

"Like you had to."

"I just worry about you, that's all."

"That was one of the nice things about Ed. He never worried about me."

That stops me. "What a weird thing to say."

"Is it? Makes perfect sense to me, but then I'm a drug addict."

"Look, let's just go eat, okay? That was the plan."

She runs one hand across my cheek. "I can't. Marcie's okay, but your grandma makes me want to OD."

She leans precariously, and I hold her up. "What's going on, anyway?"

"Oh, I just . . . I don't know exactly. Partly it's those fucking meetings. All those burnouts do is play Can You Top This. One guy says he got so wasted he woke up in Tijuana, so the next guy says he got so wasted he woke up on Mars.

"And now my mom is talking about us going shopping together. She wants to get matching outfits so people will think we're sisters. And I don't sleep worth a shit anymore, so I'm taking her Halcion."

"I thought you weren't supposed to use any kind of drugs."

"And then there's that."

"What?"

"You don't trust me."

"Colleen, you're loaded now."

"Sweetie, I've got a little buzz on. There's a difference." She takes a deep breath, coughs, and rubs her chest. "So that's the long version of what's going on. The short version is this: I'm not having any fun."

"Is that what you were having that day out in the parking lot—fun? You could hardly walk. You spent three days in the hospital with an IV in your arm."

She nods. "I'm not going to smoke that much anymore." She makes a big curving motion with one hand. "Just enough to smooth out the edges." Then she turns, seizes me, and puts her forehead against mine. She links her hands behind my neck. All I can do is look down and see her tiny skirt and precarious shoes. "That's the deal, by the way," she whispers. "We can still, you know, call each other and fool around and go to movies and stuff. But I'm going to be a little buzzed sometimes." She steps back abruptly. "And I'm a little buzzed now, so I'm going dancing." She holds out her hand. "You can come. It'll be, well, fun."

"You know I can't." I point toward the gallery. "Marcie helped with all this. And we have to take Grandma home."

"I'll be at the Aorta. You know where that is."

I try to put my arm around her. "We'll give you a ride. We'll drop you off." God, I sound desperate.

"No, no, no. That's okay. I'll go with . . ."

"Nick."

"They're all named Nick, aren't they? Ever notice that?"

I watch her sway toward the Pontiac Firebird at the curb. The inevitable Nick leans on it, smoking. When she gets closer, he pushes away and opens the door.

And then I wish I had a camera, because a really beautiful shot composes itself: the palm tree on the left leans just like Nick. On the right hangs an enormous moon, the kind in old prints of sleigh rides.

I see Colleen's high heels disappear into the car, catch a glimpse of her long, white legs. Then the driver folds himself into his side of the car and they speed away.

"Benjamin!"

I make myself turn around. There stands my grandmother in her pashmina shawl.

"Benjamin, we're ready."

I feel for the slip of paper Amy gave me. I look at my picture taped to the gallery window.

"Okay," I say. "I'll be right there."